我是傑克，
超跩萬事通

文◎安德魯・克萊門斯
譯◎陳雅茜　圖◎唐唐

國家圖書館出版品預行編目（CIP）資料

我是傑克,超跩萬事通 / 安德魯.克萊門斯（Andrew
  Clements）文; 陳雅茜譯; 唐唐圖. --初版. --臺北市:
遠流, 2014.03
    面;　公分. --（安德魯.克萊門斯; 15）
  譯自 : Jake Drake, know-it-all
  ISBN 978-957-32-7378-3（平裝附光碟片）

874.59   103002706

安德魯・克萊門斯15

我是傑克，超跩萬事通

文 / 安德魯・克萊門斯　譯 / 陳雅茜　圖 / 唐唐

主編 / 林孜懃　編輯協力 / 盧珮如、丘瑾　內頁設計 / 邱銳致
行銷企劃 / 陳佳美　出版一部總編輯暨總監 / 王明雪

發行人 / 王榮文
出版發行 / 遠流出版事業股份有限公司　台北市南昌路2段81號6樓
電話：(02)2392-6899　傳真：(02)2392-6658　郵撥：0189456-1
著作權顧問 / 蕭雄淋律師
輸出印刷 / 中原造像股份有限公司
□ 2014年 3 月 1 日　初版一刷
□ 2020年10月30日　初版六刷

定價 / 新台幣260元　（缺頁或破損的書，請寄回更換）
有著作權・侵害必究　Printed in Taiwan
ISBN 978-957-32-7378-3
遠流博識網 http://www.ylib.com　E-mail:ylib@ylib.com
遠流YA讀報粉絲團 https://www.facebook.com/yaread

進入兒童的大人世界

實踐大學應外系講座教授

陳超明

在《傑克與魔豆》的童話故事中，聰明伶俐的傑克（Jack），運用智慧，巧奪巨人的財富；而在現今的校園裡，不同的傑克（Jake），也面臨不一樣的巨人，正要開始現實生活的冒險之旅。

當自己故事的主人翁

每個人小時候，大都擁有聽大人說故事或自己讀故事的喜悅！沉浸在故事的幻想世界裡，不管是小飛俠彼得潘在森林飛舞，還是孫悟空作弄不同妖魔鬼怪，或傑克與巨人間的最後對抗，我們小小的心靈，都暫時脫離父母的嘮叨、學校作業的負擔、隔壁小胖的霸凌，愉快的當自己的主人翁。

從另一面看事情，問題就解決了

故事永遠是我們心靈的好夥伴；好的故事，更是我們展現想像力的好場所！將故事結合現實面，這套【我是傑克】系列，帶我們進入「兒童的大人世界」。我們跟隨著主人翁傑克，有如巨人世界的傑克般，進入各種學校與生活冒險。聰明善良的傑克不斷摸索，發掘事情的另一面，找到破解的方法。

大家常常說，小孩是個無憂無慮的天使。真的是如此嗎？這些故事顛覆了我們大人的看法。回想一下，我們小時候在學校裡，是不是也要面對很多成長的挑戰：不同階段的霸凌、太聰明或太愚蠢的煩惱、同學老師的排擠或另眼相看？故事裡，傑克願意面對自己的問題，也認識自己有限的能力。故事中常不經意的批評大人的輕忽與便宜行事，往往成為小孩世界的夢魘。

迷人的說故事能力

作者是個說故事高手，以第一人稱的敘述觀點進入小孩的世界，勾劃出這些學校的夢魘，更製造層層高潮，吸引我們閱讀：傑克如何打敗超級霸凌者？傑克如何對抗「師寶」的封號？傑克如何鍛鍊自己的智力？傑克又如何發現老師的另一面？小孩的「成熟」，對照大人的「無知」，正是這些故事迷人的地方。誠如傑克自己所說，他一直搞不懂，學校這些每天在教導他們的大人不是應該很聰明、很厲害嗎？為什麼他們始終沒辦法解決校園霸凌的問題呢？不管是大人，還是小孩，來閱讀這些小孩或大人間的精采互動，都會覺得非常有趣！

如何閱讀本系列作品

【我是傑克】不僅是教導小孩如何找到解決問題的方法，更是

學習語言的好故事書。作者簡潔的語言與故事間的精采轉折，都是本書成功的地方。遠流出版，保留其英文原文，是個非常聰明的作法。我們可以閱讀中文，了解故事情節，也可以回頭看英文，品味這些簡潔語言帶來的美感與魅力。例如 "I tried to smile and nod at him, but I know I looked kind of spooked, because I was spooked. And Link could see I was spooked. And he liked it. And that's when I knew I was in big bully-trouble." 短短四句，重複 spooked，一方面交待傑克成為霸凌對象的過程，一方面也點出其內心的驚慌。這種精采句子到處可見，值得細讀。

這是一系列情節緊湊、語言簡潔、啟發性強的少年故事，大人、小孩都可一起閱讀，不但可以幫助你學習語言，也可以協助你好好面對問題、解決問題！

6

【推薦導讀二】

給讀【我是傑克】的你們

兒童文學作家
幸佳慧

親愛的，我猜，你拿到這本書，可能是父母長輩買來或找來給你的，也可能是同學推薦的。不管怎樣，我們因此在這裡、這一頁相遇。你正讀著字，讀著我這個推薦導讀人寫的字……我的工作就是好好的向你介紹這系列的四本書，就像你的一個好朋友發現了好東西時，會急著和你分享一樣。

安德魯‧克萊門斯是美國一位擅長寫學校故事的作家，他總能以學生觀點捉摸到學校生活的各種面相，所以他寫的故事在美國很受歡迎。因為小讀者不會覺得作家藉機說道理（我完全可以體會你們聽說教故事的心情，那感覺就像一朵花好端端的被強行帶到沙漠裡一樣，令人煎熬難受），而是懂得你們的處境或心理，隨著你們

的眼睛去感受學校會發生的事情。那種感覺，就像作家透過文字的魔法讓你們變成一尾尾小魚，跳入小溪、滑入大海去自在悠游，卻同時能帶領你們看到特別的新景物。

【我是傑克】這系列講的是一個小男生在他小學不同年級所發生的故事，每本書就像一片片不同的海域，讓小魚兒帶著熟悉的安全感與新鮮的好奇心去探索。

《我是傑克，霸凌終結者》是在說鎮上新來的一個小孩是個小惡霸，而且他偏偏挑中傑克當他欺負的對象。這讓傑克有機會回想自己為何老是成為惡霸磁鐵的原因，並且激起他要當霸凌終結者的鬥志。不知道你有沒有被霸凌或霸凌別人的經驗？我幼稚園時，有好幾次被霸凌的經驗，那種恐怖心情，一直到現在還記著呢。你們呢？有思考過為何會發生霸凌，發生了要怎麼應對嗎？

《我是傑克，完美馬屁精》這本也是說著我們都熟悉的情境。

我自己就學期間，從幼稚園到博士班都不喜歡那種會巴結老師或討老師歡心的學生，也就是老師眼中的寵物，同學眼中的馬屁精。不過，有時候你偏偏就會被某個老師盯上，他會對你很好，開口閉口都是你，這讓你很困擾，因為你不想被老師馴服、被同學排擠，你想和同學們同一國，卻不知道該怎麼辦？喔，相信我，那可沒那麼簡單，絕對比把期末考考好還要難，但卻有意思極了！

另外，你有沒有過這種經驗？眼前有個大賽，比的正是你的長項，而且獎品非常非常吸引你，為了得獎，你於是進入了一種六親不認、全力以赴，卻又疑神疑鬼的狀態。整個過程很煎熬，考驗著你和家人、同學的關係，也衝擊著自己對自己的信心，但同時一路上也可能出現意外而有趣的路口，等著你轉彎過去！如果有，那你

一定要讀《我是傑克，超跩萬事通》這一本。

另一本《我是傑克，天才搞笑王》也描述了我小時候在學校經歷過的事，就是你明明知道在老師面前「乖乖的」便可以沒事，但你還是忍不住「搞怪」。你也知道下一刻因此要惹禍上身，卻意外觀察到老師們有異狀，然後你才慢慢發現，其實他們有另一個不是老師的身份存在。這個新發現讓你重新看待自己和大人的關係，也才知道原來上學這件事有好笑、溫柔與不為人知的一面呢！

總之，我很努力的向你們介紹這四本書有意思且吸引人的地方，希望你接下去有機會翻完它們，並回過頭來評評我分享的話有沒有道理。若覺得沒道理，那也很好，這樣你就可以開始寫你想分享給其他小讀者的推薦導讀了，我可是很樂意拜讀的！

名家好評推薦

乖巧、伶俐，帶著一點膽怯，卻又總是強自鎮定的傑克，和我兒子正好同年，今年十歲，四年級。而且，有點小聰明的性格也有那麼一點類似呢！所以，每當我看到傑克在學校裡遇到麻煩與困擾時，忍不住也會想像，當我兒子遇到同樣情形時，他會怎麼辦？

克萊門斯的作品活潑逗趣，貼近小朋友的想法與經歷，讀來輕鬆愉快，又引人入勝。【我是傑克】系列以中英雙語方式出版，拉長了閱讀年齡層，讓高年級的孩子也可以把它當成一本練習英文的讀本，是相當值得收藏的好書喔！

——親子作家　陳安儀

1 圈套

我是傑克，全名叫傑克·德瑞克，現在四年級，十歲。

有件事我得招認一下：那就是我這輩子一直很迷電腦。

我的第一部電腦是黑白螢幕的經典款老麥金塔，我在上面玩「聰明兔」、「神奇數學」，在螢幕上畫畫，還玩「坦克大戰」。那時候，我甚至還不認識字呢！

接著，我們家有了一台彩色大螢幕的麥金塔，我在上面

玩「俄羅斯方塊」、「上海」、「接龍」和「幽靈」遊戲。在我四歲時，收到一個耶誕節禮物是遊戲搖桿，我最好的朋友威利也是，所以不論何時，只要威利來我家，我們都會一起玩電腦遊戲。並不是說我們一直在玩電腦，因為我媽在我家訂立了「一天只能玩一個小時」的規定，但威利和我幾乎每天都會把那個小時填滿。

後來電腦開始變得超級快，我在上面玩起「虛擬鼓手」，然後是「模擬城市」和「模擬螞蟻」，還有「高爾夫巡迴賽」及其他十幾種遊戲。接著，網際網路來到我家，突然間，我可以用電腦做些非常神奇的事，它就像一扇魔法窗戶。

我會說這些，是因為如果不說，接下來的故事就會讓我

看起來很混蛋。但我不是混蛋，大部分時間都不是。我只是

真的很喜歡電腦。

剛開始上幼稚園時，我們教室裡有一部電腦，老師看我

對電腦很在行，就讓我使用。我甚至還教其他小朋友怎麼用

電腦，不過凱文和瑪莎除外。他們不喜歡我教他們電腦或者

其他的任何事。

就像我之前提到的，我現在十歲，所以已經有點時間去

了解一些事，而其中有件事我很確定，那就是沒有比當個萬

事通更糟的事了。

可別弄錯我的意思。我其實挺聰明的，也喜歡當個聰明

人；況且幾乎所有我認識的小孩也都很聰明。

不過有些小孩就是一定要證明自己很聰明，而且總是如此。他們不僅要聰明，還必須是最聰明的一個。瑪莎和凱文就是那樣。

上幼稚園的時候，瑪莎・麥考和凱文・楊還算友善，只要我不試著告訴他們有關電腦的事。因為當我試著告訴凱文怎麼使用繪圖軟體畫形狀時，他就會說：「我知道那個。」可是我不覺得他真的知道。當我試著告訴瑪莎怎麼把小貓圖案列印出來時，她就會說：「我可以自己來。」

但大多數時間，凱文和瑪莎還算友善，因為在幼稚園大部分是遊戲時間。

可是升上一年級後，學校變了。突然之間，答案有了對錯，而凱文和瑪莎對於得到正確答案，簡直是著了迷。

但還有更糟的。他們兩人都想**第一個**得到正確答案，這就像是他們覺得上學是參加電視上的益智競賽節目，只要第一個得到正確答案，就能贏得大獎。反正，他們兩個都變成了萬事通。

我們一年級的導師是格蘭姆斯小姐。她每一次問問題，瑪莎就會全身開始搖來晃去，大力揮手，並且說著很大聲的悄悄話，像是：「喔，喔！我知道！我知道！我知道！」

當瑪莎在那裡「喔，喔」的時候，凱文就會一副整個身體快被自己的手從椅子上拉起來、而且要被拉上天花板的樣子，好像他的手臂自己長了腦袋之類的。

這種感覺很糟，可是當凱文和瑪莎每件事都想得第一，格蘭姆斯小姐卻喜歡這樣。她喜歡看誰能第一個解出數學問題，也喜歡讓拼字測驗一百分的人，排在午餐或休息隊伍的最前面。一年級就像一場大比賽，而格蘭姆斯小姐會對勝利的人微笑，對失敗的人皺眉頭。

當格蘭姆斯小姐在班上問問題時，大部分時候會第一個叫瑪莎。如果瑪莎動作太慢或不知道答案，接著就會輪到凱文。如果凱文搞砸了，她才會叫其他人。

我想我知道格蘭姆斯小姐為什麼每一次都叫瑪莎和凱文，我想，那是因為她自己也是萬事通那一型的人。我敢打賭，她一年級的時候就和瑪莎一樣。

到了二年級並沒有改善太多。唯一一件好事是，二年級導師布萊托太太和格蘭姆斯小姐不一樣。布萊托太太不希望上學變成一場大比賽，所以幾乎很少點名那兩位萬事通。

一整年下來，布萊托太太常把這些話掛在嘴邊：「凱文、瑪莎，請看看班上其他同學，他們也有很好的想法。現在請你們把手放下來。」

那並無法阻止凱文和瑪莎。「喔，喔」聲和搖擺的手從來不曾放棄。

但在去年，升上三年級時，事情變得失控了。我猜有部分是我的錯。

而我三年級的導師斯納文太太呢？她和這件事有一點關

係，我們的校長卡普太太也是。

另外還有來自汪奇超級電腦專賣店的這個人——雷尼·科

多先生，他是影響重大的關係人。

因為在我三年級那年的某一天，雷尼·科多先生來到我

們學校，而且雷尼·科多先生告訴我，他有禮物要送給我。

那是個超棒的禮物，而且是我渴望很久的。

只不過有個小圈套，因為每次都至少會有一個小圈套。

這個圈套就是：我必須先做一件事，雷尼·科多先生才

可能把我渴望的那個超棒的禮物送給我。

我得先把自己變成「萬事通」——傑克·德瑞克。

2 大新聞

每當學校有大事要發生，孩子們總是到最後才知道。首先，校長、老師和其他大人會把每一件事情弄清楚，然後才會告訴我和我的朋友們。這似乎不大公平，但事情的經過就是這樣。

耶誕假期前的某個星期二早上，三、四、五年級的學生被叫去集合。我和其他所有三年級學生一起坐在最前面。

校長看起來很巨大。卡普太太本來就長得高，但那天早上，她穿了一身綠衣站在講台上，看起來就像一根巨無霸綠芹菜。

講台上還有其他人，是一位我不曾見過的男士，身穿黃色的休閒西裝外套，脖子上別著一個紫色底綠圓點的領結。

那是我第一次看到黃色的休閒西裝外套，以及有著綠圓點圖案的紫色領結。我想那個人可能是在馬戲團工作。

他坐在一張摺疊椅上，大腿上面橫擺著一大捲紙。禮堂裡很吵。接著，卡普太太舉起兩根手指，並且靠向麥克風。

真不該讓卡普太太使用麥克風的，她根本不需要。學校裡每個孩子都知道她的吼聲有多大。每當卡普太太一吼，彷

佛所有磁磚都會從地板上脫落下來，並開始胡亂飛舞。

沒有人想聽卡普太太吼叫，尤其是對著麥克風。所以大

約只花了一秒鐘，禮堂裡就安靜了下來。

卡普太太說：「同學們，早安。」

接著她暫停了一下。

於是我們所有人都說：「卡普太太，早安。」

然後卡普太太說：「今天早上，我有個好消息要公布。

汪奇超級電腦商店的人和我們的教育委員會談好了，在一個

月內，我們學校的媒體中心將會出現二十部全新的電腦。二

十部新電腦，這不是很棒嗎？」

卡普太太暫停了一下，禮堂裡所有的孩子和老師開始鼓

掌。有些五年級學生開始歡呼，大喊著「耶！」「好極了！」和「讚！」之類的話。

卡普太太只好再度舉起兩根手指。禮堂裡立刻安靜下來。

接著她說：「但是今天早上，我只叫三、四、五年級的班級來集合，是為了另一個理由。那就是，我們學校要在一月的倒數第二週舉辦一場科學展覽！」

卡普太太再度暫停。

但這次沒有人鼓掌。

她接著說：「這是戴普雷小學第一次舉辦科展，對我們所有人來說，都是全新的經驗。為了讓你們對首次科展活動有更多了解，我想介紹一下雷尼·科多奇先生，他是汪奇超級

電腦商店的經理。科多先生。」

那位穿著黃色休閒西裝外套和紫色底綠圓點領結的男士站了起來。他忘了擺在大腿上的紙捲，所以紙捲掉在地上，從舞台前方滾落。許多孩子開始大笑。於是卡普太太站回麥克風後面，笑聲立刻停止了。

斯納文太太從前排的座位上站起來，撿起大紙捲，遞回給那位男士。

雷尼‧科多先生比卡普太太矮了一截，所以他得把麥克風調低。接著他說：「謝謝你，卡普太太。很高興能夠來到這裡。」

科多先生雖然嘴裡那麼說，看起來卻一點也不高興。他

滿頭大汗，手上的紙捲也在顫抖。我猜我們看起來很可怕，所以他講話很快，似乎想早點結束。

「在汪奇超級電腦商店，我們熱愛孩子。在汪奇超級電腦商店，我們覺得只要能夠讓孩子對科學、電腦和未來產生興趣，不論何時都不嫌早。也因此，汪奇超級電腦商店對於能夠贊助戴普雷小學第一屆的年度科展，感到很光榮。」

這時科多先生舉起那個大紙捲，把它展開。那是一張海報，上面寫著「汪奇盃第一屆小學年度科學展覽」。

海報上面最大的字是「汪奇盃」，而且這整張海報上下拿顛倒了。

會場上爆出一些笑聲，又很快停止，因為科多先生繼續

說下去。他已經不再害怕，現在說起話來就像電視上賣車的傢伙。

「在真實的世界裡，也就是你們將在其中生活、學習和未來工作的世界，要有好的表現才能得到獎勵。所以汪奇超級電腦商店現在要提供一個**大獎**，給在三、四、五年級中做出最佳科展研究作品的同學！」

當你說出「**大獎**」這兩個字時，孩子們一定會注意聽。

現場變得好安靜，我幾乎可以聽見汗水滑下科多先生額頭的聲音。他看到我們正在注意聽，於是放慢了速度。

「沒錯，第一屆汪奇盃年度科展將會準備三**個**大獎。你們想不想知道這些大獎各是什麼？」

禮堂裡的每個孩子全都異口同聲大喊：「想！」

所以科多先生朝麥克風靠得更近，並且喊了回來：「那

我就告訴你們！三年級、四年級、五年級最棒的科展研究作

品將會得到的大獎就是……擁有超多功能的全新布朗騰十二

系統電腦！」

我不敢相信！這三個月以來，布朗騰十二電腦的廣告不

斷出現在各個電視頻道，以及每一份報章雜誌上。我在廣告

看板上看過，甚至連公車車身上都有。

布朗騰十二是我一直求爸媽買給我的電腦。它有最快的

速度，還有最酷的遊戲和最佳的連線系統。

那是我夢想中的電腦。

我身邊的孩子都在拍手，說著「好棒！」「酷！」「耶！」之類的話。

然後我注意到凱文，接著又注意到瑪莎，他們兩人和我坐在同一排。

凱文和瑪莎並沒有拍手，也沒有說話。

凱文和瑪莎坐得直挺挺的，他們正在思考。

他們已經在計畫要怎麼贏得那部布朗騰十二電腦──**我的電腦！**

當卡普太太要大家安靜下來時，我仍然繼續觀察，而且我看得出其他孩子也在做同樣的事。孩子們開始在思考和計畫了。

卡普太太又說了些其他事，但我沒聽到。我也在思考。

因為我知道，在我和我那台超快、超酷的電腦之間，只有一件事擋著，那就是其他三年級約一百名學生的腦袋。

但我有個直覺，我真正必須擔心的腦袋，只有那兩位萬事通的，也就是凱文・楊和瑪莎・麥考。

3 比賽規則

有關科展的集會結束之後，教室裡變得鬧哄哄的。

斯納文太太走進教室，她說：「請大家坐回自己的座位，我有東西要給你們。」

艾瑞克‧肯納說：「是電腦嗎？」

每個人都笑了，連斯納文太太也是。

她說：「不是，不是電腦，艾瑞克。不過**確實**是和科展

有關的消息。」

這句話讓大家很快安靜下來。

「好了，」斯納文太太說：「首先大家必須了解的是，學校沒有規定任何人一定要參加科展。你們可以自己選擇要不要參加。這會是個不錯的經驗，但不論參不參加，對你們的成績都不會有任何影響。」

斯納文太太一邊說，一邊從桌上拿起一疊資料，開始傳給大家。

她說：「這是關於科展的訊息，把這本小冊子帶回家，和爸媽一起讀。裡面有一張表格，需要你和家長簽名。要參加科展的人，請在耶誕假期之前把表格帶回來給我。第三頁

34

要特別注意，裡面說明了你可以做哪些類型的研究案，以及不該做的是哪些。」

教室裡一片死寂，只聽得見翻頁的沙沙聲。

我拿起我的小冊子開始翻來翻去。裡面總共有十頁，看起來都很無聊。所以我開始把它摺起來，這樣才能放進背包帶回家。

但這時我看到了凱文，他正靠在桌上快速閱讀著。他拿著一枝鉛筆，在紙上做著小小的記號，並且寫些註記。

接著我轉頭看向教室另一側觀察瑪莎。一模一樣，只不過她使用的是粉紅色螢光筆。

如果是平常時候，我大概只會看看瑪莎和凱文，然後自

言自語的說一句：「萬事通。」

但是那天不一樣。我抓起我的紅筆，翻開有關科展的資料，然後開始閱讀。我才不要讓那兩個孩子拿走我的布朗騰十二電腦！

接著斯納文太太說：「關於科展，有沒有任何問題？」

凱文立刻舉起手。

斯納文太太說：「是的，凱文？」

「我們可以找人合作科展嗎？」

斯納文太太開始翻閱科展的說明書。她說：「第九頁的地方有說明：『學生可獨立報名，也可找一位夥伴合作科展作品。』」

接著我舉起手來。斯納文太太朝我點點頭，所以我說：

「但如果是兩個人合作，然後得到第一名呢？兩個人能各得一個獎品嗎？」

斯納文太太又翻了翻說明書，然後她說：「第六頁有說：

『三、四、五年級每個獲勝的研究方案只能得到一個獎品。』

所以傑克，答案是不能。如果是組隊贏得第一名，我想隊員們就得想辦法共享那個獎品，或是看怎麼分。」

所以就是那樣了，我必須自己來。我才不要和任何人分我的新電腦。

斯納文太太說：「還有其他問題嗎？」

另外兩位孩子舉起手，是皮特．莫里斯和瑪莎。瑪莎先

被點到名字。

瑪莎不管說什麼，聽起來都像是在問問題。

她說：「第七頁嗎？嗯，它是說我對科展研究方案的想法必須先得到批准嗎？在開始進行前嗎？嗯，如果我想在今天就開始呢？比如說，今天回家之後呢？或是今晚呢？」斯納文太太笑了。「我想你最好等一等，先和爸媽討論過後再開始，瑪莎。別擔心，還有很多時間。」

看到了嗎？斯納文太太怎麼會說「還有許多時間」呢？又怎麼會說「別擔心」呢？那是因為斯納文太太不懂。她不了解那些萬事通總是需要正確答案，總是需要成為第一名，或者他們總是在擔心。

皮特・莫里斯的手還舉著，所以斯納文太太點他說話。

皮特是個喜歡科學的小孩。不論哪一種蟲他都認識，甚至知道牠們的怪名，以及哪一種蟲與另一種蟲有關係，還有牠們吃些什麼，以及能夠活多久。皮特真的很聰明。

皮特說：「我認為昆蟲是做科展的好題目，因為我有很多不同的蟲。昆蟲是我的嗜好，岩石也是，還有蠕蟲和植物，有時我也喜歡不同種類的猴子。所以，如果科展題目和自己的興趣一樣，這樣可以嗎？」

斯納文太太說：「那是個好問題，皮特，而答案是可以的。不過，我還是覺得你們大家必須和爸媽談一談，他們能夠幫你們決定怎麼做會最好。好了，今天有關這件事的討論

就到這裡。」

接下來是安靜的閱讀時間，所以我們全把科展的東西放在一邊，拿出圖書館的書。

除了我之外，還有瑪莎。她把科展資料放在腿上，好讓自己繼續閱讀。

我甚至不想多花力氣觀察凱文，我知道他也一定還在想著科展的事。

至於我呢？我把資料放在桌上，就墊在圖書館的書本底下，這樣我才能看到。我必須展開行動，也許在午餐之後去一趟圖書館，那樣就可以搶得先機。

因為我想成為第一名，成為最棒的。我想要贏。

而且我不只是想要贏，我是**必須要贏**。
我必須成為第一名的萬事通。

4 獵人

在午餐時間之前，我已經把有關科展的每條事項都讀過了，還讀了兩遍。我已經準備好要展開行動了。

所以等到午餐前那一刻，斯納文太太一個人坐在桌子前的時候，我走過去，有點像說悄悄話那樣向她要了一張圖書館證，說我打算午餐之後去一趟。當她一拿給我，我立刻把證件藏在手裡。

不過瑪莎還是都看到了。因為瑪莎正像看著倉鼠的貓那樣的看著我，並且立刻跳起來衝到老師的辦公桌邊。她說：

「斯納文太太嗎？圖書館證呢？我也可以要一張嗎？」

只不過瑪莎並沒有放低聲音，於是三秒鐘之後，凱文也拿到一張圖書館證。

所以就是那樣，你只能試著習慣。萬事通，通常也是個學人精。

午餐過後，圖書館就像在召開萬事通大會似的，所有聰明的孩子都聚在那裡，外加自以為聰明的孩子，還有那些希望別人覺得自己很聰明的孩子。再加上我。

我們全都在那裡，每個人都想要搶得先機。每個人都想要贏。

唯一的好處是，那裡的孩子不是全都三年級。除了我、瑪莎和凱文，其他只有三個孩子是三年級。

皮特‧莫里斯並不在裡面。我望向窗外，看到了皮特。

他正在圍籬附近的灌木叢那裡，彎腰觀察其中一根樹枝。

不過我最好的朋友威利也在圖書館。威利真正的名字叫做菲爾，但因為他姓威利斯，所以大家都叫他威利，就連他的老師也這樣叫他。威利三年級的導師是佛魯太太。

威利一看到我，立刻露出笑容來到我桌子旁。「嘿，」他說：「這不是很棒嗎？我是說那個電腦啊？真想把它擺在我房間裡。你有沒有想到什麼好主意？我想我可能會建一座橋

之類的，你知道的，就是某種巨大的東西。那你呢？你想要做什麼？」

但我只說：「聽著，威利。我現在得工作，好嗎？」

「當然，」威利說：「但我在想，也許我們可以組隊，可以做個什麼真正……你知道的，就像，真正……真的東西。」

威利對於開啟話題很在行，只不過要把句子完成就難了。

我搖搖頭。「行不通，威利。如果我們得到第一名的大獎呢？那該怎麼辦？」

威利看著我，好像覺得我瘋了。「那我們就會得到這部很酷的電腦，就那樣呀！有時可以擺在你家，有時擺在我家。一定會很棒！」

我再次搖搖頭。「我不那麼想，威利。我覺得我們最好各做各的。」

威利聳聳肩。「好呀。不過如果我贏了，我有時還是會讓你用一下我的電腦，行嗎？」

我笑著回答：「當然，那太棒了。」

但我心裡其實是這麼對自己說的：「你？想要贏科展？算了吧，威利。那個大獎是我的。」

那麼想實在不怎麼好。但是當你必須得到正確答案，而且必須是第一個，也就是必須贏的時候，你不會有太多時間去當好人。

威利離開時，我又看了一遍有關科展的資料。其中有個

部分說，科展研究方案在操作時不能使用火或酸。至於電力，只能使用電池。而且不能使用可能導致爆炸或產生煙霧的化學物質。

這些規則把許多有趣的東西都排除在外了。

小冊子裡還說，會有五名裁判。所以我試著想像科展裁判會有什麼樣的想法，但很快就覺得累了。光是要像三年級學生那樣子思考，就已經夠難了。

我抓起資料，走向已經連上網路的電腦。我坐下來，用滑鼠點選「搜尋」，然後輸入「科展研究方案」幾個字。

兩秒鐘不到，結果就出來了。螢幕上寫著，有二十萬六千九百九十六個網頁符合我的搜尋！並且列出了前十個連結。

於是我點選一個叫做「科展小幫手」的連結，那聽起來像是正確的東西，而且真是如此，裡面有一些好東西。所以我又點選了第二個連結，而那個連結裡也有一些好點子。第三個連結也是如此，第四個、第五個都是。

接著我頓悟到一件事：每個網頁裡大概都會有好點子，那二十萬六千九百九十六個網頁統統都是！但我並不需要二十萬個點子，我只需要一個，一個**我自己**的點子。

我感到有什麼東西在我身後，於是很快轉過身。猜猜看是什麼？是凱文・楊。他已經來到我正後方，並且盯著螢幕看，我的螢幕。

「嘿！」我說：「你在做什麼，凱文？」

凱文聳聳肩。「沒事。」

我說：「那請你去別的地方沒事吧。」

凱文有著一頭紅髮，滿臉雀斑，他的眼珠子是真正的灰藍色，而且不太常眨眼睛。

凱文昂起下巴，並且說：「這裡是圖書館，我想在哪裡就在哪裡。而且你知道的，從網路上抄襲作品是違規的。」

這時瑪莎突然從某個書櫃的邊緣繞出來，站到凱文的身邊。她點點頭，腦後的馬尾跟著跳上跳下。「沒錯，凱文說的嗎？抄襲？那就像……作弊嗎？」

這讓人很難不生氣，是真的生氣。

但我只說：「什麼？你們覺得我是笨蛋嗎？我知道不能

作弊。少管閒事，你們兩個都是。你們知道現在的狀況看起來像什麼嗎？就像你們兩個正在抄襲**我的**點子，現在看起來就像這樣。」

他們離開了，我還是感到很生氣。

但之後回想起來，我感覺好多了……我是指凱文和瑪莎很注意我這件事。他們對我並不是那麼有把握，這讓我感覺很好，因為他們在擔心我，這表示我有值得他們擔心的地方。

傑克‧德瑞克擁有那些萬事通不知道的地方，而且他們兩個對這點都很清楚。

5 萬事通和一手包

那天晚上晚餐過後，我告訴爸媽有關科展的事。那時我們正在享用冰淇淋點心，媽媽和我吃的是巧克力口味，爸爸和艾比的是香草草莓。艾比是我的妹妹，比我小兩歲。所以我念三年級那時候，艾比念一年級。

我把科展的小冊子遞給我爸，他立刻就翻完了，每一頁大約看了兩秒鐘。

他說：「好……是……很合理……這很好……不錯。很棒啊，傑克，這會很有趣的。」

然後他撕下最後一頁的同意書回條，簽上自己的名字之後，把筆遞給我。「就在線上簽名吧，傑克……好了，我們現在全準備好了。所以你覺得呢？你想做火箭嗎？或者可能做個火山？那些都很有趣。還是來做行星模型？我一向很想做土星，你知道嗎？就是那個有環的行星啊？那會是個很棒的研究方案。」

在此同時，我媽開始閱讀那本小冊子，仔仔細細的讀。

艾比則是什麼也沒做，只不斷攪著她碗裡的冰淇淋。

媽媽說：「我的天啊！吉姆，你有看到第一名能得到的

54

大獎嗎？」

「嗯，當然⋯⋯嗯，是啦，」爸爸說：「第一名一向都有獎品。我贏得七年級的科展時，就得到一個不錯的獎座。但我想是我妹把那個獎座扔掉了，就在我去念大學的時候。」

我媽對我眨眨眼，然後對爸爸說：「好，你知道會有獎品，但你知道獎品是什麼嗎？」

我爸說：「嗯⋯⋯不知道，我的意思是，我不是很清楚。」

「但我知道會有獎品，所以我們要努力獲勝，對吧，小傑？例如用火箭來贏，做一些真正令人興奮的東西吧。裁判都喜歡令人興奮的作品。」

媽媽已經翻到另一頁。她斜瞄了我一眼，說：「傑克，

你為什麼不跟你爸說明一下，為什麼你不能做火箭去參加科展呢？」

我說：「那是因為第三頁有寫到，任何會燃燒、冒煙或爆炸的東西，我都不能做。」

爸爸說：「嗯……**也有**其他類型的火箭呀……像是利用水力的那種。你知道的，水火箭啊？所以，我們還是可以做火箭。」

媽媽大笑出來，並且說：「聽起來很像阿通和阿包會說的話。」

我說：「什麼意思……阿通和阿包？」

艾比的視線從她那碗冰淇淋湯中抬了起來。她說：「我

知道，是『萬事通』和『一手包』的意思。媽媽跟我說過。」

我想起來了，我以前也聽過媽媽這麼說。

有一次，爸爸不想看如何組裝新腳踏車的說明書，媽媽就說他是阿通和阿包。

還有一次，我們裝了新的車庫門開關，結果爸爸把馬達裝反就弄壞了。他沒看說明書。那件事情發生時，媽媽就說：「親愛的，有時我真希望你不要那麼阿通和阿包。」

或是當我們開車迷了路，我爸不願意停下來問路時，我也聽過媽媽說：「別當阿通和阿包。」

媽媽把小冊子遞回給爸爸，他開始閱讀。

我說：「你知道那個大獎嗎？爸，很讚喔！如果我贏得

第一名，就能得到一部布朗騰十二電腦！由汪奇超級電腦商店提供。」

爸爸說：「一整套系統？一部布朗騰十二？」

「對！」我說：「還有一整年免費上網服務！」

爸爸吹了一聲口哨。

艾比也試著吹吹看，但只是讓融化的冰淇淋流到她下巴而已。

爸爸又看了一次小冊子。他說：「嗯，我猜我們最好趕快展開行動吧，呃，傑克？」

看到了嗎？我爸是怎麼說「我們」的？他說：「……我們最好趕快展開行動……」

那個「我們」讓我擔心了起來，這應該是**我的**科展。科展的資料裡明白寫著，孩子們必須自己完成作品。

接著我又想：「如果我的作品得到第一名，爸爸卻以為他會得到一部新電腦，那該怎麼辦？」

像凱文和瑪莎那樣的孩子？我知道他們會是個問題，我已經有心理準備了。

但如果你爸爸是萬事通，還是個一手包，那該怎麼辦？

你怎麼叫自己的爸爸放手呢？又怎麼跟他說，你不想和任何人分享新電腦，連他也不行？

在這個科展計畫中，只容許一個萬事通存在。

而那個萬事通就是我。

6 怎麼辦？

吃完點心後，我拿著科展的小冊子回到房間。要怎麼選擇題目，小冊子裡面有些建議。

科學展覽的規則說，我必須使用**科學方法**，運作方式就像這樣：

先看看周遭的世界，找出有趣的現象。那叫做**觀察**。

觀察之後，試著對某個現象提出問題。那個部分叫做**提**

61

問。看起來很有道理。

接著，猜猜看問題的答案是什麼，在做科展時，這個猜測叫做**假設**。不過它仍然是一個猜測。

然後設計一些實驗方法，用來測試自己的猜測對不對。那部分叫做**方法**。

接著就是進行測試，並且把發現記錄下來。那叫做**結果**。

之後你必須判斷自己的猜測對不對。那叫做**結論**。

不過我從一開始就卡住了，我在問問題的部分遇到了麻煩。所以我繼續讀下去，科展小冊子上說：

題：

試試看把下面的空格填滿，就會是一個你可以探索的問

對──────有什麼影響？

小冊子裡提供了兩個例子：

全黑的環境　對　沙鼠的睡眠長短　有什麼影響？

洗碗精　對　小草幼苗　有什麼影響？

所以我試著填入一些自己想到的文字。

木屑　對　香草奶昔的味道　有什麼影響？

死蟑螂　對　睡覺時艾比的枕頭　有什麼影響？

紅辣椒　對　威利的花生醬三明治　有什麼影響？

我喜歡我的問題。

提問之後，你必須猜測。所以我也試了一下⋯⋯

木屑會讓香草奶昔嘗起來像⋯⋯三合板？

睡覺時艾比的枕頭上如果有死蟑螂，會⋯⋯造成大聲尖叫、瘋狂亂吼，還會讓我被禁足三週，不能看電視，也不能玩電腦遊戲。

在威利的花生醬三明治放紅辣椒⋯⋯會讓威利從椅子上

跳起來，狂灌六盒巧克力牛奶，然後在餐廳吐得一塌糊塗。

都是一些相當不錯的猜測。

但我不能再胡搞瞎搞了。

所以我躺在床上，看著天花板。我的天花板上有許多漩渦和凹凸的圖案。就像在看雲一樣，我有時能從上面看到各種東西，但那天晚上什麼都看不到，只有一大片空白。

決定科展要做什麼是件難事。會這麼困難，是因為你真正必須做的，是決定**不要**做什麼。

因為你什麼都能做，你能做的事有幾百萬種。

但是真正去做時卻只能做一件。

所以把**不要**做的事全部挑出來之後，再看看剩下的是什麼，那就是你要做的。

我從床上爬起來，走到衣櫃旁，打開最上層的抽屜。那是我的垃圾抽屜，我媽媽都這樣叫它，因為對她來說，裡面的東西看起來都像是垃圾。

然後我想到一個點子，也許看看我的那些垃圾，就可以找到靈感了，只要全部看過一遍。

於是我從背包裡拿出筆記本，翻到空白的一頁。我找出一枝鉛筆，然後看著我的垃圾抽屜，開始列起清單。

7個迴紋針

9個舊電池

1顆橘色高爾夫球

2個木製溜溜球

13條橡皮筋

18張棒球卡

3枝筆

7支不知道是哪裡的鑰匙

9顆彈珠

2顆迷你超級彈力球

1條壞掉檯燈型的拉繩

1個紅色馬蹄型磁鐵

1個迷你飛盤

1個喉糖空盒裝了1個25分加拿大幣

3個大迴紋針

1個削鉛筆器

1個扭曲的削鉛筆器

1個腳趾甲剪

1個沒有繩子的塑膠溜溜球

4台風火輪小汽車

6張威利的籃球卡

29枝彩色鉛筆

17枝蠟筆

1個塑膠放大鏡

1對骰子中的1顆

1個小鎖，沒有鑰匙

1支黑暗中會發亮的壞手錶

37個1分硬幣

1捲細電線

1個紅色印台

1把塑膠尺

1個粉紅色橡皮擦

1個釣魚浮標

1根裂開的拐杖糖

1個底片盒，裝了43顆藍珠子

3支迷你螺絲起子

1個破掉的蝸牛殼

3個紅色塑膠大頭釘

4枝短鉛筆，沒有橡皮擦

3個奶油焦糖圈

3根生鏽的螺栓

1個破洞的沙包球，藍珠子漏出來了

2片從沙灘撿來的綠玻璃

1把指甲銼刀

1個米老鼠造型的水果糖罐

1個白色橡皮擦

1根收音機天線

6個筆蓋

2張電腦磁碟片

1個迷你釘書機

1個口香糖販賣機的塑膠環

1支手電筒，不會亮

1捲透明膠帶

1條狗項圈

1個白膠的塑膠瓶

3顆灰色石頭

1把橘色把手的剪刀

1 顆眼珠，我的舊玩具貓毛毛掉的

1 台壞掉的相機

1 個小小的咖啡色玻璃瓶

3 個來自佛羅里達州的貝殼

1 個塑膠吹泡泡器

1 根大鐵釘

3 根小鐵釘，全生鏽了

1 個計算機

1 支塑膠口琴

1 個耶誕襪上掉的鈴鐺

1 個軟木塞

1 把鉗子

1 個迷你神奇畫板鑰匙圈

4 個星際大戰公仔

3 個從加菲貓腳掌掉下來的吸盤

1 條白色鞋帶

1 面圓鏡子，從媽媽化妝品上拿的

2 個沙士瓶蓋

4 條參加基督教青年會營隊贏來的彩帶

1 支舊牙刷

1 小捲白線

1 捲短捲尺

1 個遊戲組裡的沙漏

1 個鐵絲鑰匙圈

我停了下來。裡面其實還有更多東西，但我已經寫得很累，而且我不想多用一張紙；再加上我覺得好像只是在浪費時間。

我幾乎快向爸爸求救了。那可能會有危險，因為阿通與阿包之類的事。也許會很糟，但總比永遠找不到點子好。

但是在我盯著那些東西看時，突然想起一件事。

我想起以前曾在兒童雜誌裡讀過磁鐵的事，關於如何在鐵製的東西外面纏上電線，接著如果讓那條電線通電，就能變出磁鐵。

我把一大堆東西推開，找出那根大鐵釘。那根鐵釘大約有十公分長。接著，我找出那捲細電線，從鐵釘的頭開始，

把電線一圈一圈纏繞在鐵釘上面。電線並不長，不過我還是在鐵釘上纏了大約三十圈才纏完。

接著，我抓起了腳趾甲剪，把電線一端的塑膠皮撕掉一些，再找出電線另一端，也撕掉一些塑膠皮。

現在我需要電力。我把電線的一端按在電池頂端，另一端接在電池底部，然後讓鐵釘末端靠近一個小小的迴紋針。接著⋯⋯什麼事都沒發生。零。沒有。

我把鐵釘、電線和電池丟進收屜，開始把抽屜關上。

然後我想到：「嘿！你這個笨蛋！那顆電池可能已經沒電了⋯⋯再試試看！」

我在抽屜裡四處翻找，找出一顆小的方形電池，就像無線電對講機用的那種。我把電線的末端各自掛在電池上方的兩個小凸起上，然後把鐵釘移到迴紋針旁邊。**咻！**迴紋針立刻跳到鐵釘上！另外三根迴紋針也一樣，還有瓶蓋，以及指甲銼刀！

我看一看電線、電池和鐵釘，又看看懸掛在鐵釘下的東西，然後我對自己說：「很好，但這對我的科展有幫助嗎？

這只是從我的垃圾抽屜裡撈出來的蠢東西。」

我再看一下那本科展手冊，在提問的部分，它這麼說：

—— 對 —— 有什麼影響？

所以我問我自己：

「<u>電池變多</u> 對 <u>磁鐵的磁力</u> 有什麼影響？」

然後我又問自己：

「<u>電線變長</u> 對 <u>磁鐵的磁力</u> 有什麼影響？」

接著我想：

「<u>是電池變多，還是電線變長，會造成比較大的影響</u>？」

最棒的部分是，我真的很想知道答案！

你知道嗎？有時你就是可以在腦海裡看到東西，就好像它真的在那裡一樣？我當時的情況就是如此。

我可以看到一張大海報，上面寫著我的點子，另一張海

報則寫著我怎麼測試自己的點子，以及我得到的結果是什麼。

我看到我做了一些超級大磁鐵，全都掛在電池上，像學校裡的電燈一樣嗡嗡作響，而且我的磁鐵正把沉重的鐵塊吸起來。

我看到自己在科展的展場，看到裁判正在聽我解釋每一件事，而且他們在微笑。

我還看到凱文和瑪莎。他們可就笑**不**出來了。

而且我看到自己坐在房間裡，正在用全新的布朗騰十二電腦玩「Z艦隊射擊遊戲」。

簡單得很。

我只需要讓這些事情變成真的。就這樣。

7 祕密與間諜

耶誕假期來臨前的那個星期，我學到好多事。

我學到有關科展和大獎的事。我學到雷尼‧科多先生並不在馬戲團工作。我學到我渴望贏得布朗騰十二電腦。我學到我爸有時可能是個「萬事通」或「一手包」。我學到有關科學方法的事。

而且我還學到，你不會因為只有三年級，就表示你沒辦

法閱讀一些很長的辭彙。

　　就好比「電磁鐵」，這個怪名字指的是用電線、鐵和電流做成的磁鐵。這是我學到的另一件事。因為在耶誕節前那個星期的剩餘時間裡，我盡可能讀完有關磁鐵的資料。

　　我學到的另一件事就是，身為一個萬事通，也不可能真的無所不知。沒有人能夠知道**所有的事**。那太過頭了。如果你真的知道所有事，你的頭大概會爆炸或什麼的。

　　但我猜沒有人向凱文或瑪莎提過這件事。他們真的想知道所有事，總是如此。

　　但有些事他們不知道，而且他們知道自己並不知道。

　　他們不知道我的科展研究方案是什麼。

一開始，凱文試著假裝不在乎。放假的前一天，我們必須繳交同意書回條。斯納文太太要我們把回條拿到她的桌子上。我站起來，凱文跟在我後面。我看得出來他是故意的。

凱文拍拍我的肩膀。我轉過身，他一臉假笑並且說：「所以，傑克，你的科展方案要做什麼呢？」

我說：「我不想告訴任何人。」

他說：「為什麼不想？讓別人知道並沒有關係呀！像我就是在研究螞蟻。」

凱文用他灰藍色的眼珠盯著我，眼睛眨也不眨。他在等我說話，尤其是他剛剛已經把自己的方案告訴我了。

但我只是微笑並點點頭。我說：「螞蟻，很好呀，螞蟻

id=1

我是傑克，超跩萬事通

媽媽很喜歡那個瓷偶，因為她說那看起來很像艾比，所以艾

兩年前，艾比把媽媽放在架子上的一個小瓷偶弄壞了。

看到了吧！我可是很會保守祕密的。

凱文緊抿著雙唇，一臉氣憤，然後走回他自己的座位。

我說：「等到科展時我再給你看。」

凱文說：「所以是什麼呢？你在考慮什麼？」

我說：「我還在考慮。」

呢，傑克？」

凱文跟著我回到我的座位。「所以你的研究方案是什麼

納文太太。

很酷。」然後我就轉身背對他，因為我必須把我的回條交給斯

78

比也很喜歡它。

有一天，艾比把一張椅子推到架子旁邊，然後把它拿下來。當她開始玩那個瓷偶時，它的頭竟然掉了下來。

艾比哭著把瓷偶拿來給我，她擔心自己會惹上大麻煩。

我用白膠把頭黏回去，黏得很仔細，你甚至看不出來瓷偶壞了。我把瓷偶擺回架上，並且保證會守密。我辦到了。

當然，大約過了一星期之後，艾比還是對媽媽招認了瓷偶的事，媽媽甚至沒生氣。儘管如此，我還是保守了祕密。

還有一次，有個朋友和我一起參加基督教青年會營隊。

睡到半夜時，他把我叫醒，很小聲的說：「傑克，我⋯⋯我尿床了。怎麼辦？」

那種事會讓小孩子得到很難聽的綽號，所以我幫他把床單從床上拿下來。幸好睡墊是塑膠做的，所以我從箱子裡拿出多的床單，兩人合力把它鋪在睡墊上，再把溼掉的床單塞在他的床下，之後回去睡覺。

沒有人發現那件事，而且我也從來不曾透露。

別想猜那個朋友是誰，連試都別試，因為我不會說的。

絕不！那是祕密。

所以，我決定把科展研究方案也當成祕密。為什麼要告訴任何人？尤其是凱文‧楊。

而瑪莎呢？她從來沒問過，只是四處打探，而且技術很爛。我就好像有個雷達一樣，每當瑪莎試著來探我口風，我

都能分辨出來。

所以我讓她看我在做什麼，我也會讓凱文看。那是假期前的最後一天，當時正是圖書館時間。我讓瑪莎看到我借出一本有關蛇類的書。

之後，我讓凱文看到我在讀百科全書上有關鯊魚的段落。

然後我利用線上百科查詢一篇有關鼬鼠的文章，並且讓它留在電腦螢幕上一段很長的時間。我甚至做了一些筆記，而且還讓瑪莎看到。

之後，大約過了十分鐘，當凱文在印表機旁邊等候時，我列印了一篇有關囓齒類動物的文章，上面還有一大張老鼠的照片。當我去拿列印稿時，凱文面帶笑容的遞給我。

我也對他露出微笑。

圖書館時間快結束時，我看到凱文和瑪莎在說悄悄話，看起來好像在爭執。凱文大概覺得我在研究我的科展方案跟老鼠和鯊魚有關，而瑪莎大概覺得我在研究蛇類和鼬鼠。

他們不懂我在開玩笑，其實我是在研究**他們兩個**。我發現凱文讓我想到了鯊魚和老鼠的混合體，而瑪莎就像是蛇類或鼬鼠一樣。

他們不知道的是，在我背包最下面，那個黑暗又安全的地方，放著三本很棒的書：《磁鐵面面觀》、《製作磁鐵》及《贏得科展》。那三本書已經足夠幫助我贏得我的新電腦了。

因為在假期之前的那一個星期中，我所學到最棒的一件

事就是：想要做一個優秀的萬事通，並不需要知道其他人在做些什麼，也不需要知道所有的事。你只要知道得剛剛好就可以了。

而且，如果你有一個裝滿垃圾的大抽屜，也會有幫助。

8 退出

接著，耶誕假期到來。那一向是一年中我最喜歡的一段時間。在我們住的地方，幾乎每年耶誕節都會下雪。下雪加上不用上學，再也沒有比這更好的事了。

但是這個假期很不一樣。

耶誕節一早，我和艾比在樓梯頂端一起等。我是在想客廳那棵耶誕樹下的禮物嗎？不是。我的心思放在磁鐵上。

吃完豐盛的耶誕晚餐，等爺爺奶奶都回家之後，我有沒有在下午的休息時間玩全新的樂高動力機械套組呢？沒有。

我在爸爸的工作室裡四處翻找，搜尋電線和鐵塊。

一整個星期就像那樣過去了。每天我都會做一點科展的工作，看看我的書，畫一些畫。我採用科學方法，把事情記錄下來。

其中一天，我請媽媽帶我去五金行。我們買了四顆大電池，每顆都有一罐花生醬那麼重，滿滿一整罐那種。我們買了兩根我所見過最大的鐵釘，每根大約三十公分長，而且比我的食指還要粗。接著我們又去了電子零件商店買了兩大捲

86

退出

細電線。

　我的假期就像是那樣。當我不做科展的工作時，我會思考相關的事項。

　我的意思是，這一整個星期，我並沒有每分每秒都在做科展。其中一天我和威利一起去滑雪橇。我們玩得很愉快，而且沒有討論科展，一次也沒有。

　而且，我確實組裝了一個很棒的樂高機器，後來被艾比弄壞了。

　所以就算是偉大的科展，也不能毀了耶誕節。不過只差一點點。

　假期過後的那個星期，凱文從萬事通變成了愛現王。你

87

知道我有多麼努力保守有關科展的祕密吧？但凱文比我更努力，他努力讓每個人都知道並看見他的科展內容，隨時隨地。

當有孩子經過凱文的座位時，他會開始滔滔不絕的描述他的螞蟻。如果有誰想離開，他就會說：「來看看我還發現了什麼！」

凱文把他的大海報放在窗邊的桌上，就在那裡工作，並且直接把海報留在那裡讓大家參觀。那張海報很棒，真的，而且甚至還沒完成一半。

星期二在體育館時，凱文趴在牆邊地板上，開始用放大鏡觀察螞蟻。那些螞蟻排成一長排，朝著餐廳的門口前進。

當孩子們過來圍觀時，他開始告訴大家，他怎麼發現了螞蟻嗅聞的方式，以及螞蟻的眼睛和大顎怎麼運作。

凱文還帶來一些很棒的照片，是他用數位相機拍的，然後他在圖書館時間用彩色印表機列印出來。他把照片展示給大家看。

星期四，我和威利一起排隊等著購買冰淇淋三明治。我說：「所以你有趁假期開始做科展嗎？」

他說：「有呀，做了一些。不過我不要參加科展了，我們班上其他四個小孩也要退出。」

我不懂。我說：「什麼意思？」威利把紙撕開，咬下冰淇淋三明治的一角。他說：「我要退出科展，太麻煩了。除此之外，大家都知道凱文會贏。」

我還是很困惑，威利看出來了。

他說：「你看到凱文有關螞蟻的東西了，對吧？真的很棒。在我們班呢？卡爾‧伯頓的也很棒，他的主題是簡單的機械。不過我覺得凱文的比較好。」

然後我懂了，我知道凱文這一整個星期在做什麼了。

我說：「你看不出來嗎，威利？你看不出來嗎？那正是凱文想要的。他一直展示他的科展作品，就是想讓我們這些小孩退出。他設下一個陷阱，而你們全都掉進去了！」

威利聳聳肩。「是啦，我想也是。但有什麼意義呢？再做下去也沒什麼好玩的。」

威利不斷把冰淇淋從他的三明治中間擠出來，然後舔掉。

我說：「但是布朗騰十二呢？還有一整年免費的無線上網服務呢？難道你不想贏了嗎？」

威利再次聳聳肩。「我是說，當然，那很棒，但我並不是真的**需要**一部新電腦。而且從以前到現在，有誰會想打敗凱文呢？」

那讓我開始思考。而我對凱文感到愈來愈生氣。他並不是真的違反什麼規則，但他做的事看起來並不公平。

而且我也對瑪莎很生氣，因為她和凱文一樣壞。這一整個星期，她也一直在對每個人說她的計畫。她打算證明自己可以騙過小草的種子，讓它由上往下生長。

然後我開始對雷尼‧科多先生生氣。我認為大家會被科

展弄得這麼煩都是他的錯。他的新電腦讓每個人都瘋了。

然後我也很氣卡普太太和斯納文太太，還有其他所有的大人。是他們被汪奇超級電腦商店說服，才會有這個點子。

當我找不到其他人可以生氣之後，我開始對自己生氣。

我把自己變成了一個萬事通，我和凱文一樣惡劣，和瑪莎一樣狡猾。為了贏得大獎，我幾乎把耶誕節毀了。

但最糟的是，當時威利找我一起搭檔，我做了什麼？我把他趕走，叫他自己做。我把他丟進了有凱文的鯊魚池和有瑪莎的蛇窩裡。威利和我原本可以享受做科展的樂趣，兩個人一起。

星期四那一整個下午，我的腦袋不停的轉呀轉。我對整

退出

件事感到噁心透頂，接著我決定，現在只有一個辦法了。

我要忘掉凱文和瑪莎。

我要忘掉卡普太太和斯納文太太。

我要忘掉雷尼‧科多先生和他那部布朗騰十二電腦。

我也要像我的好朋友威利一樣，退出那蠢斃了的科展。

93

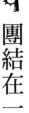

9 團結在一起

星期四下午和威利聊過之後，我想要退出科展。我是真的很想。

放學後，我在公車上完全不理任何人，一回到家就直接進我的房間。

我的桌上滿是書本和紙張。大電池、一捲捲電線和巨無霸鐵釘散落一地，還有麥克筆和海報板從床底下突出來。

我愈是看著那些東西，愈是想到威利，心裡就愈生氣。

就在那時候，我知道自己不能退出，就是不能。我不能讓凱文和瑪莎把所有人都逼退。

接著，我想到一個點子。我在桌子上翻找，直到找出那本科展小冊子。我再一次閱讀規則，然後露出這三、四個小時以來第一次的笑容。

星期五一早，我請爸爸載我去上學，這樣我就能比公車早十分鐘左右到學校。我在車上並沒有講太多話。

快到學校時，爸爸說：「所以，科展進行得怎麼樣？就在下週了，對不對？」

我是傑克，超跩萬事通

我搖搖頭。「不是，是在下下週。我想應該沒問題。」

「我能幫什麼忙嗎？雖然我沒做過電磁鐵，不過我應該知道它們的運作方式。」

我笑著說：「謝謝，不過我應該自己完成作品。規則是這麼說的。」

我們在學校正門口停車。爸爸說：「我相信你一定會做得很好。不過也許我至少可以幫忙檢查一下。」

我說：「當然，那一定會很棒。」

爸爸靠過來，親了一下我的臉。「祝你有個愉快的一天，傑克。」

我走進辦公室，請君克沃特太太准許我在第一節課的上

課鐘響前進教室。君克沃特太太是學校祕書，是個值得認識的好人。雖然校長是卡普太太，但我覺得大部分時間，學校都是由君克沃特太太在打理。因為如果你想知道任何事，找君克沃特太太談談準沒錯，除非你是惹上麻煩，那你就得跟卡普太太談了。

當我走進教室時，斯納文太太正坐在桌子前用計算機。

我想我的腳步聲一定很輕，因為當我說「斯納文太太？」時，她跳了起來，足足跳了大約三十公分高，而且還發出小聲的尖叫。「喔！是你呀，傑克。你嚇了我一大跳。」

我說：「抱歉，斯納文太太，但是我必須和你談一談。

你認識佛魯太太班上的威利嗎？他是我的朋友。我想和他搭

檔參加科展。」

斯納文太太皺起眉頭。「下下週就是科展，我覺得現在才選夥伴有點太晚了。」

我把手伸進背包，拿出科展的小冊子。我說：「裡面沒有任何地方規定必須在特定時間之前選擇夥伴，它只說必須及時報名，並說可以獨立參加，也可以找一位夥伴合作。而威利和我在耶誕節之前都已經報名了。」

斯納文太太依舊皺著眉頭。「為什麼你們過了這麼久才決定要一起合作呢？」

我說：「那是我的錯。威利一開始就想和我搭檔，但我說不要，可是我現在想要了。這樣可以嗎？」

斯納文太太深吸一口氣，然後慢慢把氣吐出來。她正在看我的小冊子。「嗯……看起來似乎沒有違反規則，所以應該可以。今天晚一點我會去辦公室拿名單改過來。」

我說：「謝謝，斯納文太太。」我走回學校的側門等公車抵達。

威利在四號公車上，但花了一點時間才下車。

「嘿，威利！過來一下！」

他看到我，揮揮手，然後擠過一大堆孩子來到我等他的地方。「嗨，傑克！」

我們走進體育館，然後我說：「你猜發生什麼事？」

「什麼事？」他說。

「我有一個新的科展夥伴了。」

威利瞇著眼睛看我。「什麼意思？誰呀？」

我咧嘴一笑。「就是你！你回到科展活動了。你就是我的夥伴！」

威利說：「不會吧！」

我說：「會！我已經跟斯納文太太報告過了，這麼做沒有違反規則或什麼的。」

威利笑了，笑容堆滿了整張臉。

接著，笑容停住，他又瞇起眼睛。「可是你說過你想要自己做科展。」

我說：「對啦，但我現在不想了。我也覺得沒那麼有趣。」

第一節課的鐘聲響起，大家開始朝門口移動。

我說：「我跟你說，午休時你去拿一張圖書證，我們可以再討論，好嗎？」

威利說：「好⋯⋯好吧。圖書館見。」然後他又露出那個滿面的笑容，是個很棒的笑容。

當你找到合作夥伴，而且還是好夥伴時，所有事情都會變得更有趣。就是會這樣。

威利和我在圖書館談過之後，我們決定要做磁鐵。他原本是想研究球的彈跳方式有什麼不同，因為威利很喜歡籃球，而且幾乎每一種運動他都愛。他對體育雖然不是很在行，卻還是很喜歡，所以他想觀察乒乓球、高爾夫球、網球

和籃球的彈跳方式。接著，他想猜測為什麼這些球的彈跳方式會不同，然後試著證明自己的猜測。

這個點子相當有趣，但威利還沒做太多研究。

當我告訴他有關電磁鐵的事，他變得超興奮。「你是說把普通鐵釘變成磁鐵嗎？」

我說：「對呀，只不過我的鐵釘是兩個巨無霸，有這麼長！還有，你知道廢棄場嗎？他們裝在起重機末端的電磁鐵可以舉起整部汽車，然後只要關上電源，**砰**！整部車就掉在地上！」

接著我告訴他，我們要做的每一件事。威利變得愈來愈興奮，他說他會問他媽媽，看能不能星期六去我家，那我們就有一整天可以做研究。

「那一定很棒。還有一件事。」我說：「這個計畫我一直都保密，尤其是不能讓凱文和瑪莎知道。」

威利緩緩點著頭，並且咧嘴笑了。「好呀，我喜歡。這表示我們知道一些他們不知道的事，對吧？」

知道我的意思了吧？威利怎麼會立刻明白我的想法呢？

我和威利就像那樣。我們是好夥伴，總是在同樣的事情上笑倒，而且當他需要幫忙或我需要幫忙時，我們就會團結在一起。

就像磁鐵黏在一起一樣。

1❸ 合作

你知道人們是怎麼說的嗎？「一人計短，兩人計長。」

嗯，沒錯，尤其其中一人是威利的時候。

星期六早上他來我家，我們立刻展開研究。首先，我把已經記錄下來的事項拿給威利看，並且告訴他，我想知道怎麼做能讓電磁鐵的磁力變得更強，是要纏上更多電線？還是加上更多電池？但我只有想法，還沒進行猜測，也就是科學

方法中的假設。

威利看看那些東西，再看看我的筆記，然後說：「增強電力會比加長電線，讓電磁鐵的磁力更強。」

我說：「你怎麼知道？」

威利搖搖頭。「我不知道呀，那是我們的假設。『增強電力會比加長電線，讓電磁鐵的磁力更強。』我們必須證明這個假設對或不對。」

現在知道兩人計長的意思了吧？不過才一分鐘，威利就已經把問題的一大部分解決了。我把那個假設寫在我們的筆記本上。接著，有趣的部分來了。我知道這聽起來可能有點奇怪，不過製作那些電磁鐵真的很有趣。

我們邊聊天邊討論，試了六種方式把電線纏在鐵釘上。

威利想到一個很棒的方式來記錄我們到底用了多少電線。

我們決定把四十五公尺長的紅色電線纏在其中一根鐵釘上，把九十公尺長的藍色電線纏在另一根鐵釘。把兩倍長的電線纏在第二根鐵釘上，也是威利的點子。依照這種方法，如果加長電線真的可以讓磁力變強，也許藍色磁鐵的磁力會是紅色的兩倍。

我們開始把電線纏到鐵釘上，電線必須纏得很緊，做起來比想像中困難。如果我得一個人完成這件事，我一定會覺得很無聊。

到了午餐時間，我們只完成了紅色電線的鐵釘，也就是

電線較短的那個。

午餐是雞湯麵和烤起司三明治。今天的午餐是由爸爸負責，因為媽媽和艾比把一些衣服拿去退還給百貨公司。奶奶送給艾比的毛衣一路垂到她的膝蓋，艾比穿起來就像《綠野仙蹤》裡的小矮人。

爸爸說：「你們在上面相當安靜，進行得如何啊？」

威利說：「我們一直在纏鐵釘上的電線。」

爸爸說：「如果太花時間，你們可以把東西拿下來工作室。我打賭我找得到工具可以讓鐵釘旋轉。那樣的話，你們只需要抓著電線，幾乎就會自動捲好。聽起來不錯吧？」

威利開始點頭，但我說：「聽起來很棒，爸，可是第二根鐵釘的纏法最好和第一根一樣。它們應該要看起來一樣。要他不管事真的很難。

我對爸爸感到有點抱歉，他真的很想幫忙。

然後我說：「不過我們纏完第二根鐵釘之後，你能幫我們看一下嗎？」

爸爸說：「當然。需要我的時候就喊一聲。」

我看得出來，我爸很高興自己能受到邀請。

威利和我完成纏電線的工作後，我們開始查閱書本，想知道該怎麼把電池串在一起。那也是我叫爸爸來的時候，因為如果大電池接錯了，可能會燒起來。而規則上說，如果有任何可能造成危險的事項，「……應該要有大人在場。」

爸爸很棒，他沒有試圖改變我們所做的任何事，也沒有說我們應該用其他方法纏電線。他並沒有變成阿通或阿包，直接告訴我們怎麼串連電池，反而是要我們想一想，然後告訴他我們想要怎麼做。

我說完之後，爸爸說：「完全正確。你們兩個自己找出答案了。」接著他就離開了。媽媽一定會以他為榮的。

威利和我決定，第一次實驗應該只用一顆電池。所以我們把紅色磁鐵兩端的電線掛在電池上，一端在正極，一端在負極。

可是我們沒有任何東西可以讓磁鐵吸，所以我們解開電線，跑到樓下的廚房。

我說：「我們需要用鋼或鐵做的東西。」

威利說：「而且我們必須知道東西的重量，因為科展的小冊子裡有說要測量每個東西，所以我們必須測量磁鐵吸起來的東西有多重。」

我打開通往地下室的門，但威利說：「等一下。」

威利已經來過我家無數次，他知道每件東西的位置。他打開櫥櫃，我立刻知道他要做什麼。他一定是要拿餅乾。但是沒有，他是從架子上抓起一個罐頭，然後說：「鮪魚！」

「鮪魚？」我說。

「對呀，」威利說：「鮪魚。這個鮪魚罐頭的重量是一百七十公克，這個湯罐頭的重量是三百零五公克，而且罐頭是

111

用鐵做的！來，拿一些吧！」

所以我抓了八個湯罐頭，他抓了四個鮪魚罐頭。

如果我把實驗的每個步驟都告訴你，你一定會發瘋的。

就是關於我們如何試著把兩顆電池接上紅色磁鐵，然後試著用鐵釘平頭的一端吸起湯罐頭，以及我們怎麼用萬用膠帶把兩個罐頭頭尾相接黏在一起，好試著一次吸起兩個罐頭；還有，我們怎麼把兩顆電池和藍色鐵釘串連在一起，然後再次試著吸起湯罐頭，還有我們怎麼把試過的每件事都寫下來，然後又怎麼串起所有四顆電池，以及……但就像我說的，這些要全部講完，你大概也瘋了。因為用講的，完全比不上和威利一起動手做這些事來得有趣。而且他會說笑話、扮鬼臉，還會提出很多很棒的點子。

那個下午過得很棒，當威利的爸爸來接他回家時，我們的科展實驗基本上已經完成了。我的意思是，接下來還有一大堆工作要做，像是畫海報，寫結論。

但威利和我都了解我們已經知道的事，並且了解我們為什麼會知道。

至於最棒的部分呢？最棒的部分是那一整個下午，我都沒想到凱文或瑪莎，也沒想到雷尼・科多先生或他的布朗騰十二電腦系統。一次也沒有。那個下午很單純就是有趣。

打從一開始，科學就應該如此，是吧？

沒錯。

11 誰是贏家？

接著，到了科展之前的週末。威利和我花了一整個星期六和星期天把海報完成。我們計畫好要對裁判說些什麼，也計畫好要怎麼說明我們的結論。

我們還必須準備好解釋我們的方法，也就是如何測試我們想法的這一部分。裁判可能會針對計畫的任何部分提出任何問題。所以你知道自己必須變成什麼嗎？你必須變成一個

115

萬事通，至少必須對自己的作品無所不知。除非你有一個像威利那樣的好夥伴，那你只需要當半個萬事通就行了。

威利和我準備好了。我們甚至還記得要買四顆新電池，好讓磁鐵運作順利。

科展在星期二舉行，我們在下午五點把作品搬到學校的體育館。那也是規則的一部分。我們有一個半小時的時間可以做準備，然後裁判會在六點半開始評審。

體育館就像爐子上的一壺水，整個地方好像在冒泡、嗡嗡嗚叫，隨時都會煮沸。

到處都是孩子，還有家長。我爸爸和威利的爸爸都來幫

我們掛海報。威利的爸爸先前去一間辦公室用品店，幫我們買了一個高大的收摺式硬紙板，大小剛好可以用來展示我們的三張海報。

地板上擺著一排排的桌子，每張都有編號。門口有張名單，每個名字旁邊都有一個號碼。我們是四十五號。

第四十五號桌很不錯，就在後面的牆邊，只不過它緊鄰著第四十六號桌，而四十六號是凱文‧楊的桌子。

要忽略凱文的作品實在很難。他和我們一樣也有三張海報，只是看起來完全不一樣。

我們海報上最大的字是用麥克筆寫的。我們用彩色鉛筆和蠟筆畫畫，用手寫字。

但凱文不是。他海報上所有的文字都是用電腦列印出來的，圖片也是。所有的紙張、文字和圖畫，全都用膠水貼在凱文的海報上。

我們也有在海報上貼一些東西。我們有貼一些圖畫，以及一張很棒的照片，照片裡廢棄場的電磁鐵正舉起一部撞壞的汽車。要把東西貼好很難，所以我們的一些圖片顯得有點凹凹凸凸，寫字的紙張也一樣。

凱文的不是這樣。我不知道他怎麼辦到的，但他的每一張圖片和所有文件全都貼得非常平坦。

我爸看著凱文的海報，然後對凱文的爸爸點點頭，說：

「很棒的海報。」

凱文的爸爸看起來很像凱文，有同樣的紅髮和藍眼珠。

他對我爸爸微笑，並說：「謝啦。我們費了不少功夫。」

看到了嗎？凱文的爸爸是怎麼說「我們」的？我看著我們附近其他作品，幾乎每一個看起來都有大人幫忙過。這似乎不太公平。突然間，我真希望曾讓爸爸幫過忙，因為在心底深處，我還是覺得能贏得布朗騰十二電腦很不錯。

凱文過來看了我們的作品一、兩次。我覺得我看到他露出小小的微笑，不過不是友善的那種笑容，而是輕蔑的那種。

但我們沒有太多時間在意凱文，還有很多事要忙。我們把磁鐵架好，再把湯罐頭和鮪魚罐頭疊好，然後把筆記本和實驗記錄攤開來。

所有事項準備就緒後，我們還剩下四十五分鐘的時間，於是我們的爸爸帶我們去吃漢堡和巧克力奶昔。食物很棒，不過威利和我相當緊張。

六點半一到，裁判開始評審。他們總共有六個人，都是來自國中的科學和數學老師。一開始，他們一群人只是沿著一排排的桌子走，然後從最後一桌，也就是第七十二號桌開始評審。我們必須等，再等，等了又等。

裁判花了很久的時間才來到我們那一排，接著又花了十分鐘，才走到凱文的第四十六號桌。

能夠在輪到自己之前先聽聽裁判怎麼問問題，這樣很不錯。凱文回答得很好，真的。他的實驗是讓螞蟻學會怎麼穿

過迷宮。他想證明如果螞蟻失去嗅覺，就會迷路。

螞蟻會在走過的地方留下氣味之類的東西，如果有隻螞蟻走出迷宮，等於留下一條路讓其他螞蟻能夠跟著走。所以當一隻螞蟻穿越迷宮之後，凱文讓另一隻螞蟻進去，那隻螞蟻走了同樣的路。接著，他用檸檬汁把迷宮塗過一遍，等檸檬汁乾掉之後，再放一隻螞蟻進去。結果第二隻螞蟻迷路了，所以凱文證明他的假設是對的。

就算凱文可能從他爸那裡得到協助，這還是個好作品。

接著輪到我們了，一位女裁判開始問問題，她請威利解釋我們想要證明什麼。威利指著海報，解釋電磁鐵的作用方式，以及我們想知道是什麼因素會造成比較大的差異，是較

長的電線，還是較強的電力。他表現得很出色。威利面帶微笑，而且聽起來好像真的很享受似的。因為他確實如此，而我看得出來，裁判也喜歡他那樣。

接著輪到我。我必須說明我們的方法。我慢慢講，一步一步來。當我說明時，威利把紅色磁鐵接上兩顆電池，並且吸起兩個鮪魚罐頭。接著他再多加兩顆電池，這次吸起了四個罐頭。

之後威利繼續講，由我把兩顆電池接在藍色磁鐵上，也就是纏繞較長電線的那個磁鐵。藍色磁鐵只用兩顆電池就吸了四個罐頭！接上四顆電池後，它吸起八個鮪魚罐頭。

我看得出裁判們喜歡我們做的事。我們得出的結果和我

們原先的設想不一樣，但我們在結論中全部解釋清楚了。我們使用了科學方法，而且那是個好實驗。

凱文也在一邊看，但我看不出他在想什麼。他並沒有微笑，也沒有皺眉，甚至沒有眨眼睛。

然後講解結束了，感覺真好。我看著威利，他臉上掛著笑，是真正的滿臉笑容。就在那時候，我知道自己並不在意是否能贏得任何東西。

裁判繼續往前走，接下來是更長更久的等待，所以威利和我去四處參觀。

很多好作品都值得一看，有關於相機的，有關於水果、蚯蚓、植物排出的二氧化碳、果蠅、化石、熱氣球、肥皂泡

和各種沙子的，還有一個真的很棒的方案是關於電吉他的聲音。以及其他更多作品。

我們找到瑪莎的桌子，但並沒有走過去，因為她看起來很傷心，而且有點生氣，就好像快哭了或是要大叫什麼的。她的海報看起來很棒，還有一個箱子。箱子旁邊開了一個窗口，裡面放著上下顛倒的蛋糕烤盤。烤盤就掛在一個小燈泡上方。從海報上可以看出來，烤盤曾經長出了一些草。

威利說：「她怎麼了？」

我聳聳肩，什麼也沒說。但我想我知道為什麼。也許是因為如果你總覺得自己必須得第一，真的太困難了。因為有許多時候，其他人就是會和你一樣好，或甚至更好。

無論如何，我們繼續向前走。我們看了三年級所有的作品方案，看完之後，我已經知道哪一組會贏了。毫無疑問。

大約過了半個小時之後，宣布結果的時間到了。每個人都走進禮堂。威利和我坐在第十排，我們的爸爸坐在我們後面。雷尼‧科多先生也在禮堂裡，所有的電腦箱子都排在講台上，這真令人興奮。

裁判先宣布五年級的贏家。艾蓮‧史東贏得大獎，她做的是有關電吉他聲音的作品。第二名是馬克‧尼克森，作品是關於溫度和肥皂泡。

四年級的贏家是查爾斯‧勒克爾，他研究不同岩石的硬度。第二名則頒給艾美‧馬汀有關葉脈的作品。

接著是三年級了。我爸把手搭在我的肩上輕捏一下。贏家是⋯⋯皮特‧莫里斯，就和我預料的一樣。

皮特的作品和昆蟲卵有關，他研究日照長度不同對卵的孵化有什麼影響。他找到一些螳螂的卵，用計時器控制燈光，然後讓卵提早兩個月孵化出來，就像用燈光欺騙了卵一樣。他還準備了一個大大的玻璃盒，裡面有二十隻左右的小螳螂正用牠們綠色的小腳在走著。

最棒的是，皮特從十月就開始做這個研究了，幾乎比卡普太太宣布科展的時間還要早三個月。他做這個作品並不是為了顯示自己比其他人更好或更聰明，也不是為了贏得新電腦，而是因為他真的希望找到事情的答案。就像我說過的，

皮特是個熱愛科學的小孩。

威利和我站起來為皮特鼓掌。然後裁判長說：「三年級的第二名是，菲爾‧威利斯和傑克‧德瑞克的電磁鐵作品。」

接著他們叫我們所有人上台去。我們必須和裁判握手，再和卡普太太及雷尼‧科多先生握手。威利和我各得到一個小小的銀色獎座，上面寫著：

第二名

第一屆戴普雷小學科學展覽

那是我贏過最棒的東西了。而且如果沒有威利在那裡滿

臉笑容的看著我，樂趣一定少了一半。

我們回到體育館，把作品拆下來。凱文和他爸爸也在第四十六號桌那裡，他爸爸看起來有點生氣。

但凱文沒有，他說：「獎座很不錯。」

我說：「謝謝，我覺得你的作品真的很棒。」

凱文說：「也許吧。你沒得到第一名真可惜。」

我說：「是呀。」

但事實上，我不覺得有那麼可惜。能得到第二名我感到很高興，原因是這樣：

你知道的，皮特的作品真的是最好的。不管怎樣，他都會贏。至於第二名呢？也許我一個人也能得到第二名，但我

不這麼想。威利做了很多事讓作品變得更好，而且我們都玩得很愉快，再加上我們都是完全靠自己完成作品的。

有關科展最棒的一點，就是它突然間就結束了。我再也不必去想它，再也不必追蹤所有的資料、電池和電線。

當我們拆掉所有東西之後，威利留下了藍色磁鐵，我留了紅色電線的那個。不論何時，我只要打開我的垃圾抽屜就能看見它。

獎座則擺在我的書架上。我把它擺在那裡是為了提醒自己再也不要變成那種人，永遠都不要，那就是「萬事通」，傑克‧德瑞克。

安德魯·克萊門斯 ⑮

Jake Drake
KNOW-IT-ALL

ANDREW CLEMENTS

Contents

CHAPTER ONE

The Catch

I'm Jake, Jake Drake. I'm in fourth grade, and I'm ten years old. And I have to tell the truth about something: I've been crazy about computers all my life.

My first computer was an old Mac Classic with a black-and-white screen. I got to play Reader Rabbit and Magic Math. I got to draw pictures on the screen, and I played Battle

Tanks. And that was before I could even read.

Then our family got a Mac with a big color monitor. And I got to play Tetris and Shanghai and Solitaire and Spectre. Then I got a joystick for Christmas when I was four, and so did my best friend, Willie. Whenever Willie came to my house we played computer games together. It's not like we played computers all the time, because my mom made a one-hour-a-day rule at my house. But Willie and I filled up that hour almost every day.

Then the computers started getting super-fast, and I started messing around with Virtual Drummer, and then SimCity, and SimAnt, and PGA Golf, and about ten other games. And then the Internet arrived at my house, and all of a sudden I could make my computer do some pretty amazing stuff. It was like a magic

window.

I'm telling all of this because if I don't, then the rest of this story makes me look like a real jerk. And I'm not a jerk, not most of the time. I just really like computers.

When I started kindergarten, there was a computer in our room. When the teacher saw I was good on it, I got to use it. I even got to teach other kids how to use it. Except for Kevin and Marsha. They didn't want me to tell them about computers or anything else.

Like I said before, I'm ten now, so I've had some time to figure out some stuff. And one thing I know for sure is this: There's nothing worse than a know-it-all.

Don't get me wrong. I'm pretty smart, and I like being smart. And almost all the kids I know, they're pretty smart, too.

But some kids, they have to prove they're smart. Like, all the time. And not just smart. They have to be the smartest. And that's what Marsha and Kevin are like.

Marsha McCall and Kevin Young were nice enough kids back in kindergarten—as long as I didn't try to tell them anything about the computer. Because when I tried to show Kevin how to make shapes with the drawing program, he said, "I know that." But I don't think he really did. And when I tried to show Marsha how to print out a picture of kitten, she said, "I can do that myself."

But a lot of the time Kevin and Marsha were pretty nice because kindergarten was mostly playtime.

But when we got to first grade, school changed. All of a sudden there were right

answers and wrong answers. And Kevin and Marsha, they went nuts about getting the right answers.

But it was worse than that. They both wanted to get the right answer *first*. It was like they thought school was a TV game show. If you get the right answer first, you win the big prize. Anyway, they both turned into know-it-alls.

Our first-grade teacher was Miss Grimes. Every time she asked a question, Marsha would start shaking all over and waving her hand around and whispering really loud, like this: "Ooh, ooh! I know! I know! I know!"

And while Marsha was going, "Ooh, ooh," Kevin looked like his arm was going to pull his whole body right out of his chair and drag it up to the ceiling, like his arm had its own brain or something.

It was pretty awful. But Miss Grimes, she liked it when Kevin and Marsha tried to be the best at everything. She liked seeing who could get done first with a math problem. She liked letting everyone with a hundred on a spelling quiz line up first for lunch or recess. First grade felt like a big contest, and Miss Grimes smiled at the winners and frowned at the losers.

When she asked the class a question, most of the time Miss Grimes called on Marsha first. If Marsha was slow or didn't know something, then Kevin got a turn. If Kevin messed up, then she would call on someone else.

And I think I know why Miss Grimes always called on Marsha and Kevin. I think it's because she's kind of a know-it-all herself. I bet she was just like Marsha back when she was in

first grade.

Second grade wasn't much better. The only good thing was that my second-grade teacher wasn't like Miss Grimes. Mrs. Brattle didn't want school to be a big contest. So she hardly ever called on the know-it-alls.

All year long, Mrs. Brattle kept saying stuff like, "Kevin and Marsha, please look around at all the other students in this class. They have good ideas, too. Just put your hands down for now."

That didn't stop Kevin and Marsha. The "ooh-oohing" and the arm waving never let up.

But last year, when I was in third grade, that's when things got out of control. And I guess it was partly my fault.

And Mrs. Snavin, my third-grade teacher? She had something to do with it. And so did the

principal, Mrs. Karp.

And so did this guy named Mr. Lenny Cordo over at Wonky's Super Computer Store. He had *a lot* to do with it.

Because Mr. Lenny Cordo came to my school one day back when I was in third grade. And Mr. Lenny Cordo told me that he had a present for me. Something really wonderful. Something I had been wishing for.

But there was one small catch. Because there's always at least one small catch.

And this was the catch : Before Mr. Lenny Cordo could give me this wonderful thing that I wanted so much, I would have to do something.

I would have to turn myself into Jake Drake, Know-It-All.

CHAPTER TWO

Big News

When something big is going to happen at school, the kids are always the last to know. First the principal and the teachers and the other grown-ups get everything figured out. Then they tell me and my friends about it. Which doesn't seem very fair, but that's how it happens.

So one Tuesday morning before Christmas

vacation, there was an assembly for the kids in third grade, fourth grade, and fifth grade. I sat up front with all the other third graders.

The principal looked huge. Mrs. Karp is always tall. But standing up on the stage that morning in a green dress, she looked like a giant piece of celery.

There was someone else on the stage. It was this man I had never seen before. He was wearing a yellow sport coat and a purple tie with green polka dots. It was the first time I had ever seen a yellow sport coat. Or a purple tie with green polka dots. I thought maybe he worked for a circus.

He sat on a folding chair, and he had a wide roll of paper lying across his lap. It was noisy in the auditorium. Then Mrs. Karp held up two fingers and leaned toward the microphone.

Mrs. Karp should not be allowed to have a microphone. She doesn't need one. Every kid in the school knows how loud she can yell. When Mrs. Karp yells, it feels like the tiles are going to peel up off the floor and start flying around.

No one wanted to hear Mrs. Karp yell, and especially not into a microphone. So it got quiet in about one second.

Mrs. Karp said, "Good morning, students."

And then she paused.

So all of us said, "Good morning, Mrs. Karp."

Then Mrs. Karp said, "I have some good news this morning. The people at Wonky's Super Computer Store have been talking to our Board of Education. And in just one month, our school is going to have twenty brand-new computers for our media center. *Twenty* new computers—isn't that wonderful?"

Mrs. Karp paused, so all the kids and the teachers in the audience clapped. Some of the fifth graders started cheering and shouting stuff like, "Yaaay!" and, "All riiight!" and, "*Awe*some!"

So Mrs. Karp had to hold up two fingers again. It got quiet right away.

Then she said, "But there's a reason that I've asked just the third-, fourth-, and fifth-grade classes to come here this morning. And that's because during the next-to-last week of January our school is going to have a science fair!"

Mrs. Karp paused again.

But no one clapped this time.

Then she said, "This is the first time we've had a science fair at Despres Elementary School, so this is something brand-new for all of us. And to tell you more about our very first science

fair ever, I'd like to introduce Mr. Lenny Cordo. He's the manager of Wonky's Super Computer Store. Mr. Cordo."

The man in the yellow sport coat and the purple tie with green polka dots stood up. He forgot he had that roll of paper on his lap. It dropped onto the floor and rolled off the front of the stage. A lot of kids started laughing. Then Mrs. Karp moved back toward the microphone, and the laughing stopped.

Mrs.Snavin got up from her chair in the front row. She picked up the wide roll of paper and handed it back to the man.

Mr. Lenny Cordo was a lot shorter than Mrs. Karp, so he had to pull the microphone down. Then he said, "Thank you, Mrs. Karp. I am so glad to be here."

That's what Mr. Cordo said, but he didn't

look that way. There was sweat all over his forehead, and the roll of paper in his hands was shaking. I guess we looked scary. So he talked fast to get it over with.

"At Wonky's Super Computer Store, we love kids. At Wonky's Super Computer Store, we think it's never too early to get kids excited about science and computers and the future. And that's why Wonky's Super Computer Store is proud to sponsor the First Annual Despres Elementary School Science Fair."

And that's when Mr. Cordo held up the wide piece of paper and let it unroll. It was a banner. It said WONKY'S FIRST ANNUAL ELEMENTARY SCHOOL SCIENCE FAIR.

The biggest word on the banner was "WONKY'S." And the whole banner was upside down.

There was a little laughing, but it stopped because Mr. Cordo kept talking. He wasn't scared anymore. Now he sounded like a guy selling cars on TV.

"In the real world, the world where all of you will live and learn and work in the future, people get rewards for doing good work. And that is why Wonky's Super Computer Store is offering a GRAND PRIZE for the best science fair project in grade three, grade four, and grade five!"

When you say those two words, "GRAND PRIZE," kids pay attention. It got so quiet, I could almost hear the sweat sliding down Mr. Cordo's forehead. He saw we were listening now, so he took his time.

"That's right. There will be *three* grand prizes for the First Annual Wonky's Science

Fair. And do you want to know what each grand prize will be?"

With one giant voice, every kid in the auditorium shouted, "YES!"

So Mr. Cordo leaned closer to the microphone and shouted back. "Then I'm going to tell you! The grand prize for the best science fair project in grade three, grade four, and grade five will be... a brand-new Hyper-Cross-Functional Bluntium Twelve computer system!"

I couldn't believe it! For the past three months, the Bluntium Twelve computer had been advertised on every TV channel. And in every magazine and newspaper. I had seen it on billboards and even on the side of a bus.

The Bluntium Twelve was the computer I had been begging my mom and dad to get. It was the fastest computer with the coolest games

and the best connections.

It was the computer of my dreams.

All around me kids were clapping and saying stuff like, "Great!" and, "Cool!" and, "Yeah!"

And then I noticed Kevin, and then Marsha. They were sitting in my row of seats.

Kavin and Marsha were not clapping. They were not talking.

Kevin and Marsha were sitting very still. They were thinking.

They were already planning how to win that Bluntium Twelve computer—*my* computer!

And when Mrs. Karp quieted everyone down, I kept looking around, and I could see that other kids were doing the same thing. Kids were starting to think and plan.

Mrs. Karp said some other stuff, but I didn't listen. I was thinking, too.

Because I saw that the only thing standing between me and my very own, superfast, super-cool computer was about a hundred other third-grade brains.

But I had a feeling that the only other brains I really had to worry about belonged to those two know-it-alls—Kevin Young and Marsha McCall.

CHAPTER THREE

The Rules

After the assembly about the science fair, our classroom was noisy.

Mrs. Snavin came in and said, "Everyone please sit in your chairs. I have something to give you."

Eric Kenner said, "Is it a computer?"

Everybody laughed, even Mrs. Snavin.

She said, "No, it's not a computer, Eric. But

it *is* some news about the science fair."

That got things quiet fast.

"Now," said Mrs. Snavin, "the first thing you all need to know is that no one has to be part of the science fair. This is something you can choose to do, or choose not to do. It will be good experience, but it will not make any difference in your grades either way."

While she was talking, Mrs. Snavin took a pile of papers from her desk and started passing them out.

She said, "This is about the science fair. You should take this booklet home and read it with your mom or dad. There is a form that you and a parent will have to sign. Bring it back to me before Christmas vacation if you are going to enter the science fair. You should pay special attention to page three. That's the page that

tells the kinds of projects that are allowed, and the kinds of projects you should not make."

It was dead quiet in the room except for the rustling of paper.

I got my booklet and started to flip through it. It had ten pages, and it all looked pretty boring. I started to fold it up so I could put it in my backpack to take home.

But then I looked at Kevin. He was hunched over his desk, reading fast. He had a pencil and he was making little check marks and notes on the pages.

Then I turned my head toward the other side of the room and looked at Marsha. Same thing, except she was using a pink Hi-Liter.

Usually, I would have looked at Marsha and Kevin and said to myself, *know-it-alls*.

But not that day. I grabbed my red pen, I

unfolded my science fair papers, and I started reading. No way was I going to let either of those kids get my Bluntium Twelve computer.

Then Mrs. Snavin said, "Are there any questions about the science fair?"

Right away Kevin's hand went up.

Mrs. Snavin said, "Yes, Kevin?"

"Can kids work together on the science fair?"

Mrs. Snavin started flipping pages in the information packet. She said, "On page nine it says, 'Students may work on a science fair project alone or with one partner.' "

Then I put my hand up. Mrs. Snavin nodded at me, so I said, "But what if two kids make a project, and it wins first place. Would both kids get a prize?"

Mrs. Snavin flipped some more pages. Then

she said, "On page six it says, 'Only one grand prize will be awarded for the winning project in grade three, grade four, and grade five.' So the answer is no, Jake. If a team won first place, I guess they would have to figure out how to share the prize or split it up someway."

So that was that. I had to work by myself. No way was I going to split my new computer with anybody else.

Mrs. Snavin said, "Any other questions?"

Two more kids put up their hands—Pete Morris and Marsha. Marsha got called on first.

Whenever Marsha talked, everything sounded like a question.

She said, "On page seven? Well, it says I have to get my project idea approved? Before I start working on it? Well, what if I want to start working on it today? Like, after school today?

And tonight?" Mrs. Snavin smiled. "I think you'd better wait until you talk with your mom or dad before you begin, Marsha. And don't worry. There will be plenty of time."

You see that? How Mrs. Snavin said "there will be plenty of time"? And how she said "don't worry"? That's because Mrs. Snavin didn't get it. She didn't understand how know-it-alls have to get the right answer. Or about how they always have to be first. Or how they always worry.

Pete Morris still had his hand up. So Mrs. Snavin called on him.

Pete's a science kid. He knows every kind of bug there is. Even their fancy names, and which bug is related to which other bug, and what they eat and how long they live. Pete's really smart.

Pete said, "I think insects would be a good

science fair topic. Because I have a lot of different bugs. Bugs are my hobby. And rocks, too. And also worms and plants. And sometimes different kinds of monkeys. So, is it okay to have your science fair project and your hobby be the same thing?"

Mrs. Snavin said, "That's a good question, Pete, and the answer is yes. But I still think you all need to talk to your moms or dads, and they can help you decide what's best for you to do. Now, that's all the time we have for this today."

Then it was quiet reading time, so we all put the science fair stuff away and got out our library books.

Except I didn't. And neither did Marsha. She put the science fair papers down in her lap where she could keep reading them.

And I didn't even bother to look over at

Kevin. I knew he was still thinking about the science fair, too.

And me? I kept the papers out on my desk. That way I could look down at them under my library book. I needed to get to work. Maybe I could go to the library after lunch. Then I could get a head start.

Because I wanted to be the first. And the best. I wanted to win.

And I didn't just want to win. I *had* to win.

I had to be know-it-all number one.

CHAPTER FOUR

Hunters

By lunchtime, I had read everything about the science fair. Twice. I was ready to work.

So I waited until just before lunch. I waited until Mrs. Snavin was alone at her desk. Then I went up and asked for a library pass for after lunch. And I kind of whispered. And when she gave me the pass, I hid it in my hand.

But Marsha saw it anyway. Because Marsha

was watching me like a cat watches a hamster. And right away, she jumped up and rushed over to the teacher's desk. She said, "Mrs. Snavin? A library pass? Could I have one, too?"

Except Marsha didn't whisper. So three seconds later, Kevin also had a library pass.

Because that's the way it is, and you have to get used to it. Know-it-alls are usually copycats, too.

After lunch, the library was like a know-it-all convention. All the smart kids were there. Plus all the kids who thought they were smart. Plus all the kids who wanted everyone else to think they were smart. Plus me.

We were all there. Everyone wanted a head start. Everyone wanted to win.

The only good thing was that not all the kids there were in third grade. Besides me and

Marsha and Kevin, there were only three other third graders.

And Pete Morris wasn't one of them. I looked out the window and I saw Pete. He was out by the bushes near the fence. He was bending over. He was looking at one of the branches.

But my best friend, Willie, was in the library. His real name is Phil, but his last name is Willis, so everyone calls him Willie, even his teachers. Willie's third-grade teacher was Mrs. Frule.

When Willie saw me, he smiled and came over to my table. "Hey," he said, "isn't it great? I mean about the computer? I would love to have that thing in my room. Got any good ideas yet? I think I might try to build a bridge or something like that, you know? Something big. How about you? What do you want to do?"

But all I said was, "Listen, Willie, I've got to get to work now, okay?"

"Sure," said Willie, "but I thought maybe we could be partners. We could make something totally... you know, like, totally... total."

Willie was great at starting sentences. Finishing them was the hard part.

I shook my head. "Won't work, Willie. What if what we make wins first prize? Then what?"

Willie looked at me like I was nuts. "Then we'll have this cool computer, that's what. We can keep it at your house some of the time, and at my house some of the time. It'll be great!"

I shook my head again. "I don't think so, Willie. I think we better just do our own stuff."

Willie shrugged. "Okay. But if I win, I'll still let you use my computer sometimes, okay?"

I smiled and said, "Sure. That'll be great."

But inside, to myself, I said, *You? Win the science fair? Forget about it, Willie. That grand prize is* mine.

Which was not very nice. But when you have to get the right answer, and you have to get it first, and you have to win, then you don't have as much time to be nice anymore.

When Willie walked away, I looked at the papers about the science fair again. There was a part that said you couldn't make a project that used fire or acid. For electricity, you could only use batteries. And you couldn't use chemicals that might explore or make smoke.

Those rules knocked a lot of fun stuff off the list.

In the booklet it said there would be five judges. So I tried to think like a science fair judge. But I got tired of that. It was hard enough

to think like a third grader.

I grabbed my papers and went over to a computer that was hooked up to the Internet. I sat down, clicked on "search," and then typed in "science fair projects."

In two seconds, I got a message. It said 206,996 Web pages matched with my search! And the first ten links were on the screen.

So I clicked on a link that said "Science Fair Helper." Sounded like the right stuff. And it was. It had some good things, so I clicked on a second link. And that second link had some good ideas, too. And so did the third link, and the fourth, and the fifth.

Then it hit me—there was probably a good idea on every page, all 206,996 of them! But I didn't need 200,000 ideas. I just needed one. I needed *my* idea.

I felt something. Behind me. I turned around real quick, and guess what? It was Kevin Young. He had come up right behind me and he was staring at the screen. My screen.

"Hey!" I said. "What are you doing, Kevin?"

Kevin shrugged. "Nothing."

I said, "Then go do nothing somewhere else."

Kevin had red hair, and his face was freckled, and his eyes were this real pale blue. And he didn't blink much.

Kevin stuck out his chin and said, "I can be anywhere I want to in the library. And you know, it's against the rules to copy a project from the Internet."

And from around the end of some shelves, suddenly Marsha was standing there next to Kevin. She nodded her head so her ponytail bobbed up and down. "That's right, what Kevin

said? About copying? How it's, like, cheating?"

It was hard not to get mad. Real mad.

But all I said was, "What? Do you think I'm stupid? I know not to cheat. Just mind your own business, both of you. You know what things look like right now? It looks like you two are copying ideas from *me*, that's what it looks like."

They left, and I was still pretty mad.

But when I thought about it later, I felt better... about Kevin and Marsha watching out for me, I mean. I was something they weren't so sure about. It made me feel good because if they were worried about me, that meant I was worth worrying about.

Jake Drake was something those know-it-alls didn't know about, and they both knew it.

CHAPTER FIVE

K-I-A/D-I-A

That night after dinner I told my mom and dad about the science fair. We were having ice cream for dessert. Mom and I had chocolate, and Dad and Abby had vanilla and strawberry. Abby's my little sister. She's two years younger than I am. So back then, when I was in third grade, Abby was a first grader.

I handed the science fair booklet to my

dad. Right away he flipped through it. He looked at each page for about two seconds.

He said, "Okay... yeah... that makes sense... this is good... fine. Great, Jake. This'll be a lot of fun."

Then he ripped the permission slip off the back page. He signed his name and handed his pen to me. "Just sign on the line, Jake... there you go. Now we're all set. So what do you think? You want to make a rocket? Or maybe a volcano? Those are a lot of fun. Or maybe a model of a planet? I always loved making Saturn, you know? The one with all the rights? That's a great project."

Meanwhile, my mom started reading the booklet. Carefully.

Abby wasn't doing anything except stirring her ice cream around and around in her bowl.

Mom said, "My goodness! Jim, did you see

that there's a prize for first place?"

"Well, of course... well, sure," Dad said. "There's always a prize for first place. When I won my seventh-grade science fair, I got a nice trophy. But I think my sister threw it out when I went to college."

My mom winked at me. Then she said to Dad, "Okay. You know there's a prize. But do you know what the prize is?"

My dad said, "Well... no, I mean, not exactly. But I know there's a prize, so we'll try to win it—right, Jackey? Like with a rocket, something really exciting. The judges love exciting projects."

Mom had flipped to another page. She looked sideways at me and said, "Jake, why don't you tell your dad why you will not be making a rocket for the science fair."

I said, "That's because on page three it says

I can't make anything that burns, or smokes, or explodes."

Dad said, "Well... there *are* other kinds of rockets... like the kind that use water power. You know, a water rocket? So, we could still make a rocket."

Mom laughed and said, "That sounds like something a K-I-A/D-I-A might say."

I said, "What's that mean... K-I-A/D-I-A?"

Abby looked up from her ice-cream soup. She said, "I know. It means Know-It-All/Do -It-All. Mommy told me."

And I remembered that I had heard Mom say that before.

One time Dad wouldn't read about how to put a new bicycle together. Mom said he was being a K-I-A/D-I-A.

And when we got a new garage door opener,

it broke because Dad hooked the motor on back-
wards. He didn't read the instructions. When
that happened, Mom said, "Dear, sometimes I
wish you weren't such a K-I-A/D-I-A."

Or when my dad wouldn't stop and ask for
directions when we were lost in the car? I heard
Mom say, "Don't be a K-I-A/D-I-A."

Mom handed the booklet back to Dad, and
he started reading.

I said, "You know the prize? It's amazing,
Dad. If I win first prize, I get a Bluntium Twelve
computer! From Wonky's Super Computer Store."

Dad said, "A whole system? A Bluntium
Twelve?"

"Yeah," I said, "and a year of free Internet
service, too!"

Dad whistled.

And then Abby tried to whistle, too. But

instead, some melted ice cream drooled down her chin.

Dad looked at the booklet again. He said, "Well, I guess we had better get right to work on this, eh, Jake?"

See that? How my dad said "we"? He said, " ... *We* had better get right to work ... "

That "we" got me worried. This was supposed to be *my* science fair. Right in the science fair booklet it said that kids had to do their own work.

And then I thought, *What if Dad thinks he's going to get a new computer when my project wins first prize?*

Kids like Kevin and Marsha? I knew they were going to be a problem. I was ready for that.

But what if your dad is a K-I-A—and a

D-I-A, too?

How do you tell your own dad to keep hands off? And that you don't want to share your new computer with anyone—not even him?

On this science fair project, there was only room for one K-I-A.

And that was me.

CHAPTER SIX

What to Do

After dessert, I took the science fair booklet to my room. It had some ideas about choosing what to do.

The rules said I had to use *the scientific method*. Which works like this:

First you look around the world and see something interesting. That's called *observation*.

After you look around, you ask a question

about something. That part's called the *question*. Which makes sense.

Then you make a guess about the answer. When you do a science fair project, your guess is called a *hypothesis*. But it's still a guess.

Then you plan out some trials to test and see if your guess is right or wrong. That part is called the *method*.

Then you do your testing, and you write down what you find out. That's called the *result*.

And then you have to tell if your guess was right or wrong. That's called the *conclusion*.

But I was stuck way back at the beginning. I was having trouble with the question part. So I kept reading and the science fair booklet said:

Try filling in these blanks to make a question you want to explore:

What is the effect of _____ on
_____ ?

And then it gave two examples:

What is the effect of dishwasher soap on
grass seedlings ?
What is the effect of total darkness on how
much gerbils sleep ?

So I tried filling in some words of my own.

What is the effect of sawdust on the taste of a
vanilla milkshake ?
What is the effect of a dead cockroach on
Abby's pillow at bedtime ?
What is the effect of a red hot pepper on
Willie's peanut butter sandwich ?

I liked my questions.

And after you ask a question, you have to make a guess. So I gave that a try too:

—Sawdust would make a vanilla milkshake taste like... plywood?

—A dead cockroach on Abby's pillow at bedtime would... cause loud screams and a lot of yelling, and make me be grounded with no TV or computer games for three weeks.

—And a red hot pepper on Willie's peanut butter sandwich would... make Willie jump up from his chair, drink six cartons of chocolate milk, and then throw up all over the cafeteria.

Pretty good guesses.

But I had to stop messing around.

So I lay down on my bed and looked at the ceiling. My ceiling has all these swirls and ridges. It's like looking at clouds. Sometimes I can see all kinds of stuff up there. But that night I didn't see anything. Just a big white blank.

Deciding what to do for a science fair is hard. It's hard because what you really have to do is choose what *not* to do.

Because you could do anything. You could do millions of different things.

Except you can only do one thing.

So after you choose all the stuff *not* to do, then you look at what's left over. And that's what you do.

I got up and went over to my dresser and opened the top drawer. It's my junk drawer. That's what my mom calls it because it all looks

like junk to her.

And then I got an idea. Maybe I could find an idea by looking at my junk. All of it.

So I grabbed my notebook from my backpack.

I opened it to an empty page. I found a pencil. Then I looked into my junk drawer and I started making a list.

7 paper clips

3 big paper clips

9 old batteries

1 twisty pencil sharpener

1 orange golf ball

1 toenail clippers

2 wooden yo-yos

1 plastic yo-yo with no string

13 rubber bands

4 Hot Wheels

18 baseball cards

6 of Willie's basketball cards

3 pens

29 colored pencils

7 keys that I don't know what
   they fit

17 crayons

9 marbles

1 plastic magnifying glass

2 mini-superballs

half a pair if dice

1 piece of chain from a broken
   lamp

1 little lock, no key

1 red magnet shaped like a
   horseshoe

1 broken glow-in-the-dark watch

1 mini Frisbee

37 pennies

1 empty Altoids tin with 1
Canadian quarter

1 roll of thin wire

1 red stamp pad

1 fingernail file

1 plastic ruler

1 Mickey Mouse PEZ holder

1 pink eraser

1 white eraser

1 fishing bobber

1 piece of a radio antenna

1 cracked candy cane

6 pen caps

1 film container with 43 blue
beads

2 computer disks

3 mini-screwdrivers

1 mini-stapler

1 broken snail shell

1 plastic ring from a gum ball

machine

3 red plastic pushpins

1 flashlight, doesn't work

4 short pencils, no erasers

1 roll of Scotch tape

3 butterscotch Life Savers

1 chain dog collar

3 rusty bolts

1 plastic bottle of white glue

1 Hacky Sack with a hole, blue
beads leaking out

3 gray stones

2 pieces of green glass from
the beach

1 pair of scissors with orange
handles

1 mini Etch-A-Sketch on a key
ring

1 eye off my old toy cat Fluffy

4 Star Wars action figures

1 broken camera

3 suction cups off of Garfield's
paws

1 small, brown glass bottle

1 white shoelace

3 little seashells from Florida

1 round mirror from Mom's
  makeup

1 plastic bubble wand

2 root beer bottle caps

1 big nail

4 ribbons I won at YMCA camp

3 small nails, all rusty

1 old toothbrush

1 calculator

1 little roll of white string

1 plastic harmonica

1 short measuring tape

1 jingle bell off of my Christmas
  stocking

1 sand timer from a game

1 cork

1 wire key ring

1 pair of pliers

And then I stopped. There was still more stuff, but I was tired of writing. Plus I didn't want to use another piece of paper. Plus I felt like I was just wasting time.

I was almost ready to go and ask my dad for help. That would be dangerous, because of that K-I-A/D-I-A thing. That might be bad, but it would be better than never finding an idea at

all.

But as I stared at all that stuff, I remembered something.

I remembered how I'd read in this kids' magazine about magnets. About how you can wrap wire around something made of iron. Then if you run electricity through the wire, it makes a magnet.

I pushed a bunch of things out of the way until I found the big nail. It was about four inches long. Then I found the roll of thin wire. Starting at the head of the nail, I began winding wire around and around, onto the nail. There wasn't that much wire. Still, I put about thirty turns on the nail before it ran out.

Then I grabbed the toenail clippers. I peeled some of the plastic cover off one end of the wire. Then I found the other end of the wire. I

peeled some plastic off that end, too.

Now I needed power. I reached into the drawer and pulled out a big fat flashlight battery. I pressed one end of the wire on the top, and the other end on the bottom of the battery. Then I put the end of the nail near a small paper clip. And... nothing. Zero. Zilch.

I threw the nail and the wire and the battery into the drawer and started to shut it.

Then I thought, *Hey, you idiot! It's probably a dead battery—try again!*

I poked around in the drawer until I found one of those small boxy batteries, like the kind from a walkie-talkie. I hooked one end of the wire to each little button on the battery. I moved the nail next to a paper clip, and *zzip!* It jumped right onto the nail! And so did three other paper clips, and so did a bottle cap, and so did

the fingernail file!

So then I looked at this wire and battery and nail. And I looked at the stuff dangling from the nail. And I said to myself, *Okay, but does this help with my science fair? This is just stupid stuff from my junk drawer.*

I looked at the science fair booklet again, at the question part, where it said:

What is the effect of _____

on_____ **?**

So I asked. I asked myself,

"What is the effect of more batteries on the power of the magnet ?"

And then I asked myself,

"What is the effect of <u>more wire</u> on <u>the power</u> <u>of the magnet</u> ?"

And then I thought,

"What makes more difference, more wire or more batteries?"

And the great part was, I really wanted to know the answer!

You know how sometimes you can just see something in your head? Just see it like it was all right there? That's how it was.

I could see this big poster telling all about my idea. And another one telling how I tested my idea, and what results I got.

I could see these big supermagnets I made.

They were all hooked up to batteries, humming like the lights at school. And my magnets were lifting up these heavy chunks of metal.

I could see myself at the science fair. I could see the judges listening to me explain everything. They were smiling.

I could see Kevin and Marsha. They were *not* smiling.

And I could see me sitting in my room. I was playing ZEE-SQUADRON STRIKE FORCE on my new Bluntium Twelve computer.

It was so simple.

All I had to do was make those things happen in real life. That's all.

CHAPTER SEVEN

Secrets and Spies

I learned a lot during that week before Christmas vacation.

I learned about the science fair and the grand prize. I learned that Mr. Lenny Cordo did not work for a circus. I learned that I wanted to win that Bluntium Twelve computer. I learned that sometimes my dad can be a K-I-A/D-I-A. I learned about the scientific method.

And I learned that just because you're in third grade, it doesn't mean you can't read some long words.

Like "electromagnets." That's the fancy name for the kind of magnets you make with wire and iron and electricity. That's something else I learned. Because the rest of that week before Christmas, I read all I could about magnets.

And another thing I learned is that a know-it-all can't really be a know-it-all. Nobody can know *everything*. There's too much. If you did know everything, your head would explode or something.

But I guess nobody ever told that to Kevin and Marsha. They really wanted to know everything, all the time.

But there was something they didn't know. And they knew they didn't know it.

They didn't know what my science fair project was.

At first, Kevin tried to pretend he didn't care. The day before vacation, we had to turn in our permission slips. Mrs. Snavin told us to bring them to her desk. I stood up, and Kevin got in line behind me. I could tell he did it on purpose.

Kevin tapped me on the shoulder. When I turned around, he gave me this fake smile and said, "So, Jake, what are you doing your project on ?"

I said, "I don't think I want to tell anybody."

He said, "Why not? It doesn't matter if people know. I'm doing mine on ants."

Kevin stared at me with his pale blue eyes. He didn't blink. He was waiting for me to tell. Especially since he had just told me what his

project was.

But I just smiled and nodded. I said, "Ants. Yeah, ants are cool." And then I turned away because I had to hand my slip to Mrs. Snavin.

Kevin followed me back to my table. "So what's your project, Jake?"

I said, "I'm still kind of thinking about it."

Kevin said, "So what is it? What are you thinking about?"

I said, "I'll show you at the science fair."

Kevin pressed his lips together and made a mad face. Then he walked back to his own table.

You see, I'm a good secret keeper.

Two years ago, Abby broke a little china statue my mom had on a shelf. Mom loved it because she said it looked like Abby. That's why Abby loved it, too.

One day Abby pushed a chair over to the

shelf and she took it down. When she started playing with it, the head broke off.

Abby brought it to me. She was crying. She was afraid she would get in big trouble. I used some white glue to put the head back on. I was very careful. You couldn't even tell it was broken. I put it back on the shelf. And I promised I would keep it a secret. And I did.

Of course, about a week later, Abby told Mom about the statue herself. And Mom wasn't even mad. Even so, I kept the secret.

And then there was the time a friend of mine was at the YMCA camp with me. In the middle of the night he woke me up. He whispered, "Jake... I... I wet my bed. What should I do?"

That's the kind of thing a kid can get a bad nickname for. So I helped him get the sheet off his bunk. It was a plastic mattress, so that was

good. I got my extra sheet out of my trunk, and we put it on the mattress. Then we stuck the wet sheet under his bed and went back to sleep.

No one ever found out, and I never told.

And don't even try to guess which friend it was, because I'm not telling. Ever. It's a secret.

So I decided my science fair project was going to be a secret, too. Why tell anybody? Especially Kevin Young.

And Marsha? She never asked. She just snooped. And she was lousy at it. It was like I had radar. I could always tell when Marsha was trying to spy on me.

So I let her see me work, and I let Kevin see me, too. It was during our library period on the last day before vacation. I let Marsha see me check out a book on snakes.

Then I let Kevin see me looking at stuff

about sharks in the encyclopedia.

Then I use *Encarta* to look up an article about weasels, and I left it on the computer screen a long time. I even took some notes. And Marsha saw me.

Then, ten minutes later, when Kevin was waiting at the printer, I printed out this article about rodents with a big picture of a rat. When I went to get it, Kevin handed it to me with a smile.

And I smiled back.

Near the end of the library time, I saw Kevin and Marsha whispering together. They looked like they were arguing. Kevin probably thought my project was about rats and sharks, and Marsha probably thought I was studying snakes and weasels.

They didn't get my joke. What I did was study *them*. And I had discovered that Kevin

reminded me of a cross between a shark and a rat, and Marsha was like a snake and a weasel.

What they didn't know was that in the bottom of my backpack, down in a safe dark place, I had three great books: *All About Magnets*; *Magnets You Can Make*; and *Winning Science Fair Projects*. And those three books were enough to help me win my new computer.

Because the best thing I learned that week before vacation was this: To be a good know-it-all, you don't have to know what anybody else is doing. And you don't need to know everything. You just have to know enough.

Plus it helps if you have a big drawer full of junk.

CHAPTER EIGHT

Dropouts

Then it was Christmas vacation. That's always been my favorite time of year. Where we live, there's almost always snow at Christmas. And there's nothing better than snow plus no school.

But this vacation was different.

On Christmas morning I was waiting at the top of the stairs with Abby. Was I thinking about all the presents under the tree in the living

room? No. I was thinking about magnets.

And after the big Christmas dinner, and after Gram and Grampa went home, did I play with my new LEGO motor kit for the rest of the afternoon? No. I dug around in Dad's workshop. I was looking for wire and pieces of iron.

And it was like that all week. Every day I did some work on my project. I read my books. I made some drawings. I used the scientific method and I wrote things down.

One day I had Mom take me to the hardware store. We bought four big batteries. Each one was as heavy as a jar of peanut butter—a full one. We bought two of the biggest nails I had ever seen. They were about a foot long, and thicker than my pointer finger. And then we went to RadioShack and bought two big spools

of thin wire.

That was what my vacation was like. When I wasn't working on my project, I was thinking about it.

I mean, I didn't work on it the whole week, not every second. One day I went sledding with Willie. We had a great time, and we didn't talk about our projects, not even once.

And I did build this amazing LEGO machine. Which Abby wrecked.

So even a big science fair project can't ruin Christmas. But it came pretty close.

The week after vacation, Kevin went from being a know-it-all to a show-it-all. You know how I worked to keep my project a secret? Kevin worked even harder to show and tell everyone about his. All the time.

If kids walked past Kevin's table, he would

start telling all about his ants. And if they tried to walk away, he'd say, "And look what else I found out!"

Kevin worked on a big poster at the table by the windows. He just left it lying there for everyone to see. The poster was great, it really was—and it wasn't even half done.

In the gym on Tuesday, Kevin lay down on the floor by the wall. He started looking at some ants with a magnifying glass. They were in a long line, marching toward the door to the cafeteria. When kids came around, he told about how he had found out the way ants smell things. And how their eyes and jaws work.

And Kevin brought these amazing pictures. He took them with a digital camera. He printed them out on the color printer during library period. He showed them to everybody.

On Thursday I was waiting in line with Willie to buy ice-cream sandwiches. I said, "So did you start your project over vacation?"

He said, "Yeah, I got some done. But I'm not going to be in the science fair. And four other kids in my class, they're quitting, too."

I didn't understand. I said, "What do you mean?" Willie peeled back the paper and bit off a corner of his ice-cream sandwich. He said, "I quit the science fair. It's too much trouble. Besides, everybody knows Kevin's going to win."

I was still confused, and Willie could tell.

He said, "You've seen Kevin's stuff about ants, right? It's really good. And so is Karl Burton's stuff. In my class? His project is about simple machines. But I think Kevin's is better."

And then I got it. I got what Kevin had been

doing all week.

I said, "Don't you see, Willie? Don't you see? That's what Kevin wants. He's been showing off his science project so kids like us will drop out. He set a trap, and you walked into it!"

Willie shrugged. "Yeah, I guess so. But what's the point? It wasn't any fun to work on."

Willie kept squeezing the ice cream out of the middle of his ice-cream sandwich so he could lick it off.

I said, "But what about the Bluntium Twelve? And a whole year of free Internet? Don't you want to win that?"

Willie shrugged again. "I mean, sure. That would be great. But I don't really *need* a new computer. And who wants to just try to beat Kevin all the time?"

That made me think. And I got madder and

madder at Kevin. He didn't really break any rules, but what he was doing didn't seem fair.

And I got mad at Marsha because she was as bad as Kevin. All week long she had been telling everyone about her project, too. She was going to prove that she could fool grass seeds into growing upside down.

And then I got mad at Mr. Lenny Cordo. I thought it was all his fault that everyone was so upset about the science fair. Everyone was going nuts about his new computers.

And then I got mad at Mrs. Karp and Mrs. Snavin and all the other grown-ups. They were the ones who let Wonky's Super Computer Store talk them into this whole idea.

And when I ran out of other people to get mad at, I got mad at myself.

I had turned myself into a know-it-all. I

had gotten as mean as Kevin and as sneaky as Marsha. I had practically ruined Christmas so I could win the big prize.

But, worst of all, back when Willie wanted to be my partner, what did I do? I sent him off on his own. I threw him into the shark tank with Kevin and into the snake pit with Marsha. Willie and I could have had fun working on a project. Together.

All Thursday afternoon my thoughts went around and around. I got sick of the whole mess. And I decided there was only one thing to do.

I was going to forget about Kevin and Marsha.

I was going to forget about Mrs. Karp and Mrs. Snavin.

I was going to forget about Mr. Lenny Cordo. And his Bluntium Twelve computer.

I was going to quit the stupid science fair, too, just like my best friend, Willie.

CHAPTER NINE

Sticking Together

After I talked with Willie on Thursday afternoon, I felt like quitting the science fair. I really did.

I didn't talk to anyone on the bus after school. When I got home, I went right to my room.

Books and papers were spread all over the top of my desk. I had big batteries and spools of wire and giant nails spread around on the floor.

I had markers and poster boards sticking out from under my bed.

The more I looked at all that stuff, and the more I thought about Willie, the madder I got.

And right then, I knew I couldn't quit. I just couldn't. I couldn't let Kevin and Marsha push everyone out of the way.

Then I got an idea. I looked around on my desk until I found the science fair booklet. Then I read the rules again. And for the first time in three or four hours, I smiled.

On Friday morning, I had my dad drive me to school. That way, I got there about ten minutes before the buses. I didn't talk much in the car.

When we were almost there, Dad said, "So, how's the science fair coming? It's next week, right?"

I shook my head. "Nope. It's the week after. And I guess it's okay."

"Anything I can help with? I've never made electromagnets, but I think I understand how they work."

I smiled and said, "Thanks, but I'm supposed to do the work myself. It says that in the rules."

We pulled up at the front door of the school. Dad said, "I'm sure you're doing a terrific job. But maybe I could at least look things over."

I said, "Sure. That'd be good."

Dad leaned over and gave me a kiss on the cheek. "Have a great day, Jake."

I went into the office and asked Mrs. Drinkwater for permission to go to my room before the first bell. Mrs. Drinkwater is the school secretary. She's a good person to know. Even though Mrs. Karp is the principal, I think

Mrs. Drinkwater runs my school most of the time. Because if you want to find out anything, you talk to Mrs. Drinkwater. Unless you're in trouble. Then you talk to Mrs. Karp.

When I got to my room, Mrs. Snavin was sitting at her desk using a calculator.

I guess my shoes were too quiet, because when I said, "Mrs. Snavin?" she jumped about a foot and let out this little squeal. "Oooh!—It's you, Jake. That gave me a fright."

I said, "Sorry, Mrs. Snavin. But I have to talk with you. You know Willie, my friend in Mrs. Frule's class? I want to be partners with him for the science fair."

Mrs. Snavin frowned. "The fair is the week after next. I think it's a little late to be choosing up partners."

I reached into my backpack and pulled out

the science fair booklet. I said, "It doesn't say anywhere in here that you have to pick partners by a special time. It just says that you have to sign up on time, and it says you can work by yourself or with one partner. And Willie and I both signed up before Christmas."

Mrs. Snavin was still frowning. "Why has it taken this long to decide you want to work together?"

I said, "That's my fault. Willie wanted to be partners right at the start, but I said no. But now I want to. So will it be okay?"

Mrs. Snavin took a deep breath and let it out slowly. She was looking through my booklet. "Well... it doesn't seem to be against the rules. So, it'll be all right. I'll get the master list from the office and change it later today."

I said, "Thanks, Mrs. Snavin." Then I went

back to the side doors to wait for the buses.

Willie was on bus four, but it was a while before he got off.

"Hey, Willie! Over here!"

He saw me and waved. He moved through the crowd of kids to where I was waiting. "Hi, Jake!"

We walked into the gym, and I said, "Guess what?"

"What?" he said.

"I've got a new partner for the science fair."

Willie looked at me and squinted. "What do you mean? Who?"

I grinned. "You! You're back in the science fair. You're my partner!"

Willie said, "No way!"

And I said, "Way! I talked with Mrs. Snavin already, and it's not against the rules or any-

thing."

Willie smiled this smile that almost covered his whole face.

Then the smile stopped, and he squinted again. "But you said you wanted to work by yourself."

I said, "Yeah, but now I don't. I wasn't having much fun, either."

The first bell rang, and everyone began to move for the doors.

I said, "Tell you what. Get a pass to go to the library for lunch recess, and we can talk about it, okay?"

Willie said, "Yeah... okay. See you in the library." And then he smiled his big smile again. It's a great smile.

When you have a partner to work with, and it's a good partner, everything is more fun. It

just is.

After Willie and I talked at the library we decided to work on the magnets. He had been making a project about how different balls bounce. It's because Willie loves basketball and almost every sport. He's not very good at sports, but he still loves them. So he wanted to observe Ping-Pong balls, golf balls, tennis balls, and basketballs bouncing. Then he wanted to guess why they bounced in different ways, and then try to prove it.

It was kind of an interesting idea, but Willie hadn't done much with it.

When I told him about the electromagnets, he got all excited. "You mean a regular nail turns into a magnet?"

I said, "Yeah, only I've got two giant nails this long! And you know at a junkyard? They

have electromagnets on the end of a crane that can pick up whole cars, and when they shut off the power, BAM, the whole car falls to the ground!"

Then I told him about everything we had to do. And Willie got more and more excited. He said he would ask his mom if he could come over on Saturday. Then we could work all day on it.

"That'll be great. And there's one more thing," I said. "I've been keeping the project a secret. Especially from Kevin and Marsha."

Willie nodded slowly and began to grin. "Yeah. I like it. That means we know something that they don't know, right?"

See what I mean? How Willie got the idea right away?

Me and Willie are like that. We're good

partners. We laughed at the same kinds of stuff, and when he needs help or I need help, we stick together.

Like magnets.

CHAPTER TEN

Teamwork

You know how people say "two heads are better than one"? Well, it's true, especially if the other head is Willie's head.

When he came over to my house on Saturday morning, we got right to work. First, I showed Willie what I had written down. And I told him how it was my idea to see what made a magnet more powerful: more wire or more batteries. I

had the idea, but I hadn't a guess about it yet. In the scientific method, that's called the hypothesis.

Willie looked at the stuff, and he looked at my notes. Then he said, "More electricity makes an electromagnet stronger than more wire."

I said, "How do you know that?"

Willie shook his head. "I don't. That's our hypothesis. 'More electricity makes an electromagnet stronger than more wire.' We have to prove whether that's true or false."

See what I mean about two heads? In a minute, Willie had a big part of the problem all worked out. I wrote the hypothesis in our notebook. Then came the fun part. I know that might sound weird, but making those electromagnets was really fun.

We talked and we argued about stuff, and

we tried six different ways of winding wire on the nails. And Willie figured out a great way to keep track of how much wire we were using.

We decided to put 150 feet of red wire onto one of the nails. We would put 300 feet of blue wire onto the other nail. That was Willie's idea, too, to put twice as much wire onto the second nail. That way, if more wire makes a stronger magnet, maybe the blue magnet would be twice as strong.

We started winding wire onto one of the nails. We kept the wire pulled really tight. It was harder than I thought it would be. And if I'd had to do it all by myself, it would have been really boring.

By lunchtime we had only finished the nail with the red wire, the short wire.

For lunch we had chicken noodle soup and

grilled cheese sandwiches. Dad made lunch because Mom and Abby were at the mall taking some clothes back. Gram had given Abby a sweater that went all the way down to her knees. It made her look like a Munchkin.

Dad said, "It's been pretty quiet up there. How's it going?"

Willie said, "We've been winding wire around a nail."

Dad said, "If it's taking too long, you could bring your things down to the workshop. I bet I could figure out how to make the nail spin around. That way, you could just hold the spool of wire and it would almost wind itself. Sound good?"

Willie started to nod his head, but I said, "That sounds great, Dad, but we'd better do the second nail like we did the first one. They should look the same way."

I felt a little sorry for my dad. He really wanted to help. It was hard for him to keep out of the way.

Then I said, "But when we're done winding the second nail, would you look at them for us?"

Dad said, "You bet. Just give a holler when you need me."

And I could tell it made my dad feel good to be invited.

When Willie and I finished winding the wire, we looked in one of the books to see how to hook the batteries together. And that's when I called my dad. Because if you hook big batteries together wrong, it can start a fire. And it said in the rules that if anything might be dangerous, "... an adult should be present."

Dad was great. He didn't try to change anything we were doing. He didn't say we

should wind the wire some other way. And instead of being a K-I-A/D-I-A and telling us how to hook up the batteries, he made us think about it. Then we had to tell him how we wanted to do it.

We told him, and Dad said, "That's exactly right. You guys have got it all figured out." And then he left. Mom would have been proud of him.

Willie and I decided our first trial should be with just one battery. So we hooked the wire from each end of the red magnet onto the battery—one wire to the positive terminal and the other to the negative terminal.

But we didn't have anything to lift with the magnet. So we unhooked the wires and went downstairs and into the kitchen.

I said, "We need something that's made of

iron or steel."

And Willie said, "And we have to know how much it weighs. Because it said in the science fair booklet to measure everything. So we have to measure the weight of what we pick up."

I opened the door to the basement, but Willie said, "Wait a minute."

Willie's been to my house so many times, he knows where everything is. He opened the pantry, and right away I knew what he was doing. He was going to get some cookies. But instead he grabbed a can off a shelf and said, "Tuna!"

"Tuna?" I said.

"Yeah," said Willie. "Tuna. This can of tuna weighs one hundred and seventy grams. And this can of soup weighs three hundred and five grams. And the cans are made of steel!

Here, take some."

So I grabbed eight cans of soup, and he grabbed four cans of tuna.

If I told you every step of our experiment, it would make you crazy. About how we tried two batteries on the red magnet. And then tried to see if we could pick up a can of soup with the flat end of the nail. And how we used duct tape to stack two cans on top of each other so we could try to pick up two cans. And how we hooked the two batteries up to the blue magnet and then tried to lift soup again. And how we wrote down everything we tired. And then how we hooked up all four batteries and... but like I said, if I just told it all, you'd go nuts. Because me telling it wouldn't be as fun as really doing all this stuff with Willie, and he was cracking jokes and making faces, and coming up with all

these good ideas.

It was a great afternoon. And when Willie's dad showed up to take him home, our science fair experiment was practically finished. I mean, we still had a ton of work to do. And posters to make. And conclusions to write.

But Willie and I knew what we knew, and we knew why we knew it.

And the best part? The best part was that all afternoon, I didn't think about Kevin or Marsha or Mr. Lenny Cordo or his Bluntium Twelve computer system. Not once. It had been an afternoon of pure fun.

Which is what science is supposed to be in the first place, right?

Right.

CHAPTER ELEVEN

Winners

Then came the weekend before the science fair. Willie and I spent all Saturday and Sunday finishing our posters. We planned what we would say to the judges. We planned how to explain our conclusion.

We also had to be ready to explain our method. That's the part where we tested our idea. Judges can ask any questions they want

about any part of the project. So you know what you have to be? You have to be a know-it-all, at least about your own project. Unless you have a good partner like Willie. Then you can be a know-about-half.

Willie and I were ready. We even remembered to buy four new batteries so the magnets would work just right.

On the Tuesday of the science fair, we brought our project to the school gym at five o'clock in the afternoon. That was part of the rules. We had an hour and a half to get everything ready. Then the judging would start at six thirty.

The gym was like a pot of water on a stove. The whole place felt like it was humming and bubbling, getting ready to boil over.

Kids were everywhere. And so were parents.

Both my dad and Willie's dad came alone to help us hang up our posters. Willie's dad had gone to an office store for us. He got one of those tall cardboard fold-up things. It was just the right size to hold our three posters.

There were numbered tables in rows up and down the floor, and there was a list of names by the door. Next to every name there was a number, and ours was forty-five.

Table number forty-five was a good one, right along the back wall. Except that it was next to table number forty-six. And table number forty-six was Kevin Young's table.

It was hard not to look at Kevin's stuff. He had three posters, just like ours. Except his didn't look like ours.

We had used markers to write the biggest words on our posters. We had used colored

pencils and crayons to make our drawings. We had written out our words by hand.

Not Kevin. All the writing on his posters had been printed out from a computer. And so had his pictures. All the papers and letters and pictures had been glued onto Kevin's posters.

We had glued some things onto our posters, too. We had some drawings, and a great picture of a junkyard electromagnet holding up a crushed car. It's hard to glue stuff right, so some of our pictures had some little bumps and ridges in them. And so did our writing papers.

Not Kevin's. I don't know how he did it, but every picture and all his writing was glued down perfectly flat.

My dad looked at Kevin's posters. He nodded at Kevin's dad and said, "Great posters."

Kevin's dad looked a lot like Kevin. He had

the same red hair and blue eyes. He smiled at my dad and said, "Thanks. We worked pretty hard on them."

See that? How Kevin's dad said "we"? I looked around at the other projects near us. And most of them looked like grown-ups had helped, too. It didn't seem very fair. All of a sudden I wished that I had let my dad help us. Because deep down, I still thought it would be nice to win that Bluntium Twelve computer.

Kevin looked over at our stuff once or twice. And I thought I saw him smile a little, but it wasn't a nice smile. It was a put-down smile.

But we had too much to do to think about Kevin for very long. We got our magnets wired up. We got our cans of soup and tuna stacked up. We laid out our notebooks and our method records.

And when everything was set up, we had forty minutes left over, so our dads took us out for hamburgers and chocolate shakes. The food was good, but Willie and I were pretty nervous.

At six thirty, the judges started. There were six of them, science and math teachers from the junior high school. First, they all just walked together up and down the rows of tables. Then they started at table number seventy-two, the last table. And we had to wait. And wait. And wait.

It took a long time for the judges to get to our row. Then it was another ten minutes before they got to Kevin at table forty-six.

It was good to hear the judges ask questions before it was our turn. And Kevin was good at answering them. He really was. He had done this experiment making ants learn how to go

through a maze. He wanted to show that if ants can't smell, they get lost.

Ants leave something like an odor where they walk. And if one ant goes through the maze, it leaves a trail so others can follow. So after one ant went through the maze, Kevin let another one go, and it followed the same path. Then he painted the maze with lemon juice, let it dry, and let another ant go. The second ant got lost, so Kevin proved his hypothesis was right.

It was a good project. Even if Kevin did get help from his dad.

Then it was our turn. This lady judge started. She asked Willie to explain what we wanted to prove. Willie pointed at our posters and told how electromagnets work, and how we wanted to see what made the bigger difference, more

wire or more power. He was great. Willie smiled, and he sounded like he was having fun. Because he was. And I could tell the judges liked that.

Then it was my turn. I had to explain our method. I took it slow, step by step. And while I talked, Willie hooked up the red magnet to two batteries and lifted up two cans of tuna. Then he added two more batteries and picked up four cans.

Then Willie took over talking. I hooked up two batteries to the blue magnet, the one that had more wire on it. And with two batteries, the blue magnet would pick up four cans! And with four batteries, it picked up eight cans of tuna.

I could tell that the judges liked what we were doing. Our results were different from

what we had thought they would be, but we explained it all in our conclusion just right. We used the scientific method. It was a good experiment.

Kevin was watching, too. But I couldn't tell what he was thinking. He didn't smile or frown. And he hardly even blinked.

Then it was over. And it felt great. I looked at Willie, and he had that smile on his face, the really big one. And right then, I knew I didn't care if we won anything or not.

The judges moved on. Then it was time for more waiting, a lot more waiting. So Willie and I went to look around.

There was a lot of neat stuff to see. There were projects about cameras, about fruit, earthworms, carbon dioxide from plants, fruit flies, fossils, hot air balloons, soap bubbles, different

kinds of sand, and a really great one on electric guitar sounds. And tons more.

We found Marsha's table, but we didn't go over. That's because she looked sad, and kind of mad, too, like she might start crying or yelling or something. Her posters looked great. There was this upside-down cake pan inside a box with a window cut in one side. The pan was hanging above a little lightbulb. I could tell from the posters that the pan had some grass growing from it.

Willie said, "What's wrong with her?"

I shrugged and didn't say anything. But I thought I knew why. Maybe it was because if you always feel like you have to be the best, it's hard. Because a lot of the time, someone else does just as well or even better.

Anyway, we kept walking. We looked at all

the third-grade projects. And after I saw them all, I knew which one was going to win. There wasn't any question about it.

About a half hour later, it was time for the announcements. Everyone went into the auditorium. Willie and I sat in the tenth row, and our dads sat behind us. Mr. Lenny Cordo was there, and all the computer boxes were stacked up on the stage. It was pretty exciting.

The judges announced the fifth-grade winners first. Ellen Stone won the grand prize. She'd done the project about the electric guitar sounds. And second place went to Mark Nixon for a project about temperature and soap bubbles.

The fourth-grade winner was Charles LeClerc. He had studied the hardness of different kinds of rocks. And second place went to Amy Martin's project about veins in leaves.

Then it was time for the third grade. My dad put his hand on my shoulder and gave a little squeeze. And the winner was... Pete Morris. Just like I knew it would be.

Pete had done this project about insect eggs and how different daylight hours make the eggs hatch. He had found some praying mantis eggs. He'd put some lights on a timer and had made the eggs hatch two months early. It was like he'd tricked them with the light. And there was this big glass box with about twenty baby praying mantises walking around on their little green legs.

The great thing was that Pete had started his project back in October. That was almost three months before Mrs. Karp announced the science fair. He wasn't doing the project to try to be better or smarter than anyone else. And

he didn't do it to try to win a new computer. He did it because he really wanted to figure something out. Like I said, Pete's a science kid.

Willie and I were standing up clapping for Pete. Then the head judge said, "And second prize in third grade goes to Phil Willis and Jake Drake for their project on electromagnets."

Then they called all of us up onto the stage, and we had to shake hands with the judges, and then with Mrs. Karp and Mr. Lenny Cordo. And Willie and I each got a little silver trophy that said:

SECOND PLACE
FIRST ANNUAL
DESPRES ELEMENTARY SCHOOL
SCIENCE FAIR

It was the best thing I ever won. And it wouldn't have been half as fun without Willie there, smiling his biggest smile at me.

We went back to the gym to take our project apart. Kevin and his dad were there at table forty-six. His dad looked kind of mad.

But Kevin didn't. he said, "Nice trophy."

I said, "Thanks. I thought your project was really good."

Kevin said, "I guess. Too bad you didn't win first place."

I said, "Yeah."

But really, I didn't think it was too bad. I was happy with second place. And here's why.

You see, Pete's project was the best. he would have won no matter what. And second place? Maybe I could have won second place all by myself. But I don't think so. Willie did a lot to

make the project better. Plus we had fun. Plus we did it all ourselves.

The best part about the science fair was that suddenly, it was all over. I didn't have to think about it anymore. I didn't have to keep track of all those papers and batteries and pieces of wire.

When we took everything apart, Willie kept the blue magnet, and I took the one with the red wire. Whenever I open my junk drawer now, there it is.

But the trophy is on my shelf. I keep it there to remind myself that there's one thing I never want to be again. Ever. And that's Jake Drake, Know-It-All.